THE BOBBSEY TWINS:
THE FREEDOM BELL MYSTERY

FREEDOM DAY!

A Lakeport school bus carries the Bobbsey Twins, Tanya Mirov, and their classmates to a special program at nearby Silver Town School. The girl shows them a beautiful silver plate engraved with the Liberty Bell, which Danny Rugg claims has been stolen from the local museum!

The young detectives learn otherwise. Later, when they meet Tanya's American parents and mention the shocking accusation, Papa Lasky orders the Bobbseys out of the house. A blizzard forces them to stay overnight, and the twins uncover the mysterious problems troubling Tanya and the Laskys.

After the strange disappearance and rescue of Papa Lasky, he reveals a sad story that leads the Bobbseys on a dangerous trail of clues. How they decode a carillon signal, expose a crooked scheme that almost destroys the Silver Town Mint Center, and bring a family to freedom will help fans celebrate America's big birthday year!

"Ooh-eee!" Flossie exclaimed.

The Bobbsey Twins: The Freedom Bell Mystery

By

LAURA LEE HOPE

GROSSET & DUNLAP
Publishers • New York

CONTENTS

The
Bobbsey Twins:

The Freedom Bell
Mystery

CHAPTER I

THE ATTIC'S SECRET

"IT's LOVELY, Tanya," said Nan Bobbsey to the girl beside her on the school bus. She was gazing at a silver plate on the other child's lap. "Did you bring this to America from your country?"

Both girls were brunettes. Nan had brown eyes, but Tanya Mirov's were darker, almost black.

"What's so great?" asked a voice behind them. Bert Bobbsey stood up and leaned forward to look at the plate. He was Nan's twin. They were twelve and in the sixth grade, with Tanya.

In the center of the large silver piece was the outline of a bell. Bert read aloud, "The Liberty Bell proclaims freedom throughout the land."

By this time Freddie and Flossie, the blond,

blue-eyed, six-year-old Bobbsey twins, had left their seats to see what was going on. They looked at the plate, then at Tanya.

Flossie asked, "Are you giving it to Silver Town School?"

"No, no," Tanya answered in her low, musical voice. "I am—what you say?—lend it for Freedom Day celebration. Freedom means very much to me, and your country helped me to be happier."

Nan smiled. "The U.S.A. has helped us be happier, too. On July 4th every year we celebrate our freedom. July 4th, 1976, is the two hundredth birthday of our nation."

Flossie, thinking of a giant birthday cake with two hundred candles on it, said, "We'll all sing 'Happy Birthday, America!'"

Freddie said, "And blow out all the candles!" He puffed his cheeks with air, then let it out in a whistling sound.

Tanya laughed. "I will help blow the candles!" she exclaimed, then became silent.

Freddie spoke. "Where'd you get the ding-dong plate?"

Tanya smiled. "That is my secret," she said.

"Oh please tell us," Flossie begged.

Freddie added, "We want to hear the secret."

Tanya looked out the bus window across the snow-covered fields for several seconds before answering. Finally she said, "I tell part of the secret. I find the plate in our attic."

Hearing this, a boy of Bert's age but taller, left his seat and came forward. He was Danny Rugg, a great troublemaker among the children.

Suddenly he burst out, "You didn't find that in your attic. It was stolen!"

After this, there was complete silence in the bus. Tanya clutched the plate and began to cry. Nan put an arm around her. The weeping girl murmured, "It is not true! I not steal it!"

Freddie Bobbsey was angry at Danny. He beat on the boy's back with his fists, while Flossie exclaimed, "You're a mean, bad, awful boy!"

"Cut that out!" Danny cried. "I know that plate was stolen because I saw it once before."

"Where?" several children asked.

Danny smirked. "I'm not going to tell you, but I *am* going to tell the police!" He turned and went back to his seat.

By this time the teacher in charge of the trip from Lakeport to the Silver Town School had left her place in the front of the bus and hurried back.

"What's the trouble?" Miss Widget asked. The small woman was the substitute teacher in Freddie and Flossie's class. The Bobbseys liked her, but wondered why she looked so sad most of the time.

Flossie tried to tell the teacher but got so

"That plate was stolen!" Danny burst out.

mixed up that Bert finally explained. Miss Widget frowned. She walked back to Danny. "You have made a very serious charge. Exactly what did you mean?"

"Just what I said. The Liberty Bell plate that Tanya has was stolen," Danny replied. "But I don't have to tell how I know."

Miss Widget said, "I heard you say something about telling the police. Maybe Tanya's plate only looks like one that was stolen. Promise me you will not go to the authorities until a complete examination of the plate can be made."

"Oh, I promise," said Danny, sulking.

"Thank you," the teacher said. She went to Tanya. "Please don't cry any more," she requested. "Danny isn't going to the police, and he probably is mistaken."

Tanya straightened up and dried her tears.

"You are very kind, Miss Widget." She smiled at the teacher, but she was so pale Nan was afraid the girl was ill. In a short time though color returned to her cheeks. Tanya put the silver plate into a cloth bag.

Everyone was quiet for a few minutes, then Freddie called out, "When are we going to get there? I'm tired of riding."

"Me too," Flossie added. "I've joggled enough."

"Pretty soon," Bert told them.

After that the bus went faster. It rolled quickly up a hill and down.

"Ooeee!" the smaller children cried. They giggled.

Flossie said, "It's just like a rolly-coasty!"

Those who were near windows pinned their noses against the cool panes and watched the snowy land whip past them. Suddenly a loud Pop! filled the air. The driver pressed on the brakes as the rear of the bus sank to the pavement with a hard bump.

"Ouch!" two young passengers burst out. They had hit their heads against the windows.

Miss Widget flew from her seat down the aisle toward them while a third little girl wept.

"I hurt my nose!" She cried and tried to rub the soreness away.

Nan and Bert, who were used to looking after their younger brother and sister, checked on them immediately.

"Are you okay?" Nan asked them.

Freddie was holding his arm. "I hit the metal," he said, referring to the hard rim under the window, "but I'm okay." Aside from some redness on his arm that would probably turn black-and-blue, he was fine.

"What happened?" Flossie wanted to know. She had a tight grip on the seat rail in front of her.

Bert slipped a hand over hers. "Had a flat tire, nothing more," he replied. "But never mind that. Are you all right, button nose?"

Flossie bobbed her head, yes. "But what's the matter with Miss Widget?"

The young woman was nervously pacing up and down the aisle, looking at each child. Now she stood in the front of the bus like a statue.

"Everybody keep calm. Just keep calm," she repeated. She glanced toward the driver, who was examining the flat tire. Finally she went outside.

Without saying anything, Bert followed the teacher to see if he could help. Miss Widget was about to order him back on the bus when the driver made a request.

"Son, do you suppose you could do me a favor? Could you run over to that farmhouse?" he asked, pointing to the red roof in the distance. "Call the police. Tell them what happened. I need a tow truck and another bus to get you kids to Silver Town School."

Miss Widget looked at Bert. "Do you want to go, Bert? Perhaps I ought to go instead."

The driver glanced at her, then winked at the boy to get going. In less than twenty minutes Bert had put through the call, then trekked back. A police car with two patrolmen and a bus and driver had already arrived.

Bert had pulled his coat collar up to cover his ears, but it did not keep them from turning pink. When he reached the broken-down bus, Nan stepped out of it. She twirled a wool cap on one finger.

"Brrr!" he shivered, but did not take the head covering from Nan.

"Why won't you wear this hat?" she asked her brother.

Bert did not have time to answer. Freddie, who wore the cap Mrs. Bobbsey had knitted for him, said, "He doesn't want to be a sissy, but you know what?"

Nan was not sure she wanted to ask. "What?"

"I don't want to be cold," Freddie replied, "like old brother pink ears!"

To get even, Bert scooped up some snow and sneaked up on his brother. He stuffed it against the back of Freddie's neck. The little boy squirmed and tried to brush it off.

"That'll teach you!" Bert said. He laughed but not for long.

Miss Widget's eyes pierced him with a disapproving gaze that put an end to his fun. "Bert Bobbsey," she said, "I don't know whether to thank you or spank you." But she smiled and helped Freddie brush off the snow.

The children boarded the second bus, which took them first to a nearby hospital. Those who had complained of any injury were examined immediately, then the rest.

"Where's Tanya?" Flossie asked Nan after a doctor had sent them back to the bus.

"She must be at the end of the line," said Nan. "I'll save a seat for her."

To their surprise, everyone returned except Tanya. After Miss Widget said a few words to the bus driver, he started the engine.

"Wait a minute. Wait a minute!" cried Flossie. "Tanya's not here yet!"

The little girl ran to the teacher, who talked to her softly. "Tanya is all right. She had to stay in the hospital."

Seeing the worried look on her sister's face, Nan joined her. "What's wrong?" she asked the woman.

Miss Widget shook her head from side to side. "Girls, please. You mustn't worry about Tanya and you must sit down."

On the way back to their seats Flossie told her sister what Miss Widget had said. Neither twin could think of anything but Tanya until they reached the stucco building with the name Silver Town School written over the doorway.

As they piled out of the bus and into the building, a police car pulled up. It was the same one that had come to their aid earlier.

The driver and another officer in a navy-blue

coat, stepped out. He was holding the bag containing the silver bell plate. In a loud voice he said, "Will the child who sat with Tanya Mirov please come here?"

Nan Bobbsey stepped forward. Her heart was thumping from fright. Had something happened to Tanya?

CHAPTER II

A BIG MISTAKE

"I was Tanya's seatmate," Nan told the officer.

He explained that Tanya had left the bag on the first bus. "Her name is embroidered on the cloth."

"What happened to her?" Nan asked quickly.

"The doctors wanted to examine her a little longer," he replied. "I'm sure she'll be all right soon. Will you please take this to her?"

"Yes," Nan replied, but still felt worried about her friend.

Suddenly Danny Rugg jumped up from his seat. He cried out, "Officer, you'd better open that bag and see what's inside before you give it back."

The policeman looked surprised but followed the suggestion. As he pulled out the plate with the Liberty Bell engraved on it, his eyes opened wide in astonishment.

"Um!" he exclaimed. "This looks like the valuable silver plate that was stolen from the Lakeport Museum."

"I knew it!" Danny yelled. "I saw it there several months ago."

Everyone was stunned. Bert came to stand beside his twin, followed by Freddie and Flossie. All sorts of questions went through the young detectives' minds. Did Tanya know she had a stolen plate? What was it doing in her attic? What had made her mysteriously ill all of a sudden?

The officer ran his hand over each side of the plate, asking the twins, "What do you know about this?"

Bert was first to reply. "As my sister told you, it belongs to Tanya Mirov."

Freddie and Flossie would have explained that Tanya had said she found it in the attic of her house, but Nan nudged them not to speak.

"Are you hunting for something in particular?" she asked the officer. He was still examining the edge.

To everyone's amazement, he announced, "This is not the plate we're looking for."

"It isn't?" Flossie cried. She was watching the reflection of ceiling lights on the engraved silver bell.

"No," he replied. "It sure isn't."

Bert was mystified. "How do you know?"

The policeman handed the plate back to Nan. "It doesn't have any hallmark on it. There is no small scroll-type design to identify the maker. Besides, it isn't silver."

"Then what is it?" Freddie asked.

"Ceramic with some kind of an overglaze."

Danny's head dropped when he heard this.

"You see," the policeman said, winking at the children, "the police can get fooled sometimes."

The Bobbseys wished Tanya had been there to hear the policeman. But even though her plate was not the missing one, they wondered if there could be a connection between them. The amateur detectives were intrigued that the plates looked so much alike. Was Tanya's copied from the original or from a photograph?

In the meantime Tanya was talking to a doctor at the hospital. "I had this trouble with my heart since I was a baby," she said in her pretty foreign accent. "You not going to keep me here, are you?"

The kindly man in a white coat rolled a cart

with various bottles and small instruments on it against the wall. "No, there's no need to," he replied. "You take it easy and you will be all right."

Tanya smiled sweetly. "Can you help me, doctor?" she asked. "I left something on the bus. My papa will be upset if I not bring it back."

She explained what had happened as the doctor picked up the telephone. "What is your number, dear?" he inquired, paying little attention to what she had said.

"Oh, please not tell Papa what I lost," Tanya begged. "He and Mama Lasky are my parents while I am in this country. I came here to go to school and to get well again. I not want to upset them."

The man assured her he was only calling her home to make sure someone would be there when she arrived. After a brief conversation, he slipped Tanya into her coat and led her to his car. "I pass your house. I will take you home." In less than fifteen minutes she was standing in front of a split-level frame house and ringing the doorbell.

A plump woman with sad gray eyes opened the door. "Tanya, what happened to you?" she asked before the young girl had stepped inside.

"Mama, I am all right; really, I am," she said. The woman threw her chubby arms around

"Please not tell Papa what I lost," Tanya begged.

the girl. "Are you sure? We worry about your health all the time," she added, leading her into the living room.

A low fire crackled in the fireplace. Next to it a moon-faced man, heavier than his wife, was snoring in a reclining chair.

"Why is Papa home so early?" whispered Tanya, as she unbuttoned her coat and took it off.

She tiptoed to a closet. The creaking of the floor stirred the man from his sleep. He squinted at Tanya.

"Papa, are you sick?" she asked him.

He pulled the recliner to an upright position. "Me? I am as strong as an ox," he said with a chuckle. "But you. Now you are a different story. You are no stronger, I am afraid, than a little butterfly."

Tanya sensed that something was bothering the man. Bracing herself, she told the Laskys all the events of the day. To her surprise, they did not respond to her story about the missing plate. Papa Lasky seemed to be in a daze.

"Please tell me what is bothering you," Tanya said.

Papa did not answer. His wife stared at the sparks of fire rising from the logs.

"You may not be able to stay with us much longer," she said, after taking a deep breath.

Her words stung Tanya. "Why not?" she asked. "What have I done? I will find the plate. Oh, please not send me back."

"Tanya," Papa Lasky said, rising from his chair, "we don't have a choice."

With pleading eyes, Tanya gazed into his. Mama Lasky said, "We don't want to send you back. I think of you as my own, even though you are my cousin's daughter." The woman would say no more in spite of Tanya's constant questions.

A heavy gloom came over the Lasky household. This was the reason why they did not hear the doorbell. On the second ring, however, Tanya answered it.

Gray clouds had rolled across the sky and tiny flakes of snow were falling steadily.

Tanya beamed when she saw her visitors.

"Nan, Flossie," she said, "Bert, Freddie, come in. Come in."

The twins stamped their feet to shake off the snow before entering.

Freddie removed his cap. "We wanted to return this." He handed her the cloth bag.

The missing plate!

"Oh, how wonderful!" she bubbled.

Flossie told her what had happened at school. "The police thought it was stolen," she said.

"Yeah, but——" Bert only managed to say

two words as Papa Lasky grabbed the plate from Tanya and threw it across the room onto the couch.

"Now get out of here!" he growled at the twins.

"Papa!" Tanya said with a shiver. "They are my friends!"

"I said get out of here!" the man repeated loudly.

Fearfully, Tanya clutched her American mother.

CHAPTER III

TROUBLE FOR TANYA

BEFORE Papa Lasky had another chance to order the Bobbseys out of his house, they opened the front door. A gust of wind blew heavy snow in their faces.

"Oh!" cried Mama Lasky and hurried to the door. She shut it with a bang. "Papa, you cannot send these children out into that!"

Freddie and Flossie cuddled up to their older sister and brother. "We could try to walk home," Freddie offered bravely.

"Nonsense!" said the woman.

Her husband's face flushed red. He sat down in the reclining chair again and put his head in his hands. "I don't know what came over me," he admitted. "Lately I——"

Flossie went to him and patted his arm. "It's okay," she said sweetly. "I want to be your friend."

That was enough to put a smile on Papa Lasky's face. "Please forgive me, children," he said. He pinched the little girl's rosy cheek.

Bert wondered what had caused the man's sudden outburst. Was it the sight of the plate or the mention of the theft? The young detective knew it was not the time to inquire.

Interrupting the boy's thoughts, Mrs. Lasky declared, "You will all stay to dinner. Maybe the snow will stop and we will take you home then. Telephone your mother and give her the message."

The matter was settled before the twins had a chance to object. Nan called Mrs. Bobbsey and explained.

Afterward, Tanya told the Bobbseys, "These are my American parents. I came here for medical treatment I could not have in my country."

The twins hoped their friend would tell them about her background but she did not say any more.

Instead, Mama Lasky tried to make up for her husband's rudeness. She told the twins, "Enjoy yourselves while I start supper."

Freddie leaned over to Flossie. "Want to play

a game?" But Flossie was too busy to answer. She had noticed tears forming in Tanya's eyes.

"What's the matter?" she asked her. "Can we help you? We're detectives."

Papa Lasky raised his eyebrows. *"You* are detectives? Ha-ha! Then I must be the king of England!" He laughed at his own joke.

"No fooling," said the little boy.

"Oh, Papa," Tanya said, "I not want to leave America and all my new friends. Maybe they can do something for me."

There was an urgent look in her eyes. But her American father simply dismissed her remark with a flick of his hand. Nan Bobbsey, however, was not going to let the subject drop.

"Why do you have to leave the U.S.A.?" she asked. "You don't have to if you don't want to. It's a free country!"

Tanya hesitated, then went on, "I not want to leave, but Papa Lasky says I may have to."

It was obvious he did not wish Nan to start asking him questions. He excused himself and went into the kitchen.

"Go on, Tanya," urged Flossie. "Finish the story." She curled up in a corner of the overstuffed couch.

Tanya said there was not much more to say. "My parents sent me to your country because our doctors at home could not help me. After I left, a bad man took over our government. My parents lost everything: their factory, all their money, everything."

Nan, who had taken Papa's cozy chair, wanted to know why Tanya had been sent to live with the Laskys.

Tanya's answer was, "Mama Lasky is a cousin to my mother," she said. "Now I sort of have two names and two mothers and fathers."

Flossie giggled. "We don't have two mommies and daddies, but ours have two each of us," she said.

"That is right." Tanya laughed, but the sadness did not leave her eyes. "My parents want me to stay here until things get better at home."

The twins were touched by the girl's story but did not know how they could help her.

"We want you to be like the free bell," announced Flossie.

Tanya looked puzzled. "What is that?"

"Flossie," said Nan, "you mean the freedom bell."

"Oh!" Tanya replied. "I thought it was called the Liberty Bell."

"It's all the same," Flossie insisted.

The chatter stopped as Papa Lasky returned to the living room. Freddie surprised him by asking, "Are you in big trouble?"

Bert was sure the two fine brown hairs on top of the man's bald head were standing straight up.

Mr. Lasky stared at Freddie for a second, then replied, "What a ridiculous question to ask! Of course I'm not in trouble. Why do you suggest such a thing?" He tried to keep his temper down.

Just then the aroma of food cooking in the kitchen caught Freddie's attention. For an instant he forgot why he had asked the question. He did not answer.

Bert answered instead. "We want to help Tanya stay in this country."

Papa Lasky relaxed a bit. "I appreciate your concern. Thank you, but we will take care of our own problems."

The Bobbseys had tried to uncover the reasons for the trouble in Tanya's American home, but could not. It was clear that Papa Lasky regarded the twins as mere children who were not able to help him.

When the Bobbseys were by themselves for a few moments before supper, Nan remarked, "I wish there were some way we could prove to the Laskys——"

"What?" Flossie interrupted.

Her brother Bert tapped her gently on the head. "That we can help," he said with a sigh. "I guess we need a magic formula."

An idea came to Freddie. When everyone was seated around the dining room table, he said to Papa Lasky, "I can make my supper disappear."

"Only if you eat it." The man chuckled. He

put a forkful of mashed potatoes in his mouth. "Like this," he added, after swallowing it.

The little boy shook his head. "This way," he replied. He took his napkin and flung it over his plate. "Abracadabra," he sang and swept the napkin away again with a flourish. He was disappointed to see the food still there.

Bert looked up at the ceiling in disbelief. "I can do a trick too," he said to his brother. "I can make *you* disappear."

Papa Lasky glanced at the boys as Freddie defended himself. "I saw a man do just what I did on TV!"

Now he picked up his glass of milk and held it high over Flossie's head. He tipped it slightly.

Nan cried out, "Freddie, stop that!"

He quickly replied, "I won't spill any milk. It's going to float away right before your eyes!"

A drop of the cool white liquid splashed on Flossie's nose as she looked up. She blinked. "You spilled it, Freddie!" his twin exclaimed as another drop plopped into her eye. "It's raining!" she giggled.

Instantly Nan got up from her chair and grabbed the glass from the little boy. "What has gotten into you, Freddie?" she scolded.

"I just wanted to make some magic for us," he replied good-naturedly.

Papa Lasky seemed to enjoy the scene, but he said, "You are still a baby, Freddie."

"It's raining!" Flossie giggled.

The little boy frowned. He did not like being called a baby. He sat down.

After that, supper was eaten in silence. Tanya watched her American father gulp down the last few bits of food on his plate and push back his chair before she spoke.

"I have something to confess," Tanya said in a low voice.

Everyone, including Flossie, who had dawdled over her dinner, put his silverware down.

Tanya whispered, "I stole the plate you were talking about!"

Her words startled the others. Bert asked, "From the museum? I can't believe it!"

"It's true," Tanya replied.

Mama Lasky was dumfounded. "Oh, Tanya, what are you saying? That plate was stolen during the summer. I remember the article about it in the newspaper. You hadn't even come to this country yet."

The girl remained silent. Nan wondered, "Is she trying to protect Mr. Lasky for some reason? She could be if she thinks he's guilty of the theft."

Once again the reddish color rose in Papa Lasky's face. "Enough, enough of this foolish talk!" he bellowed. "The plate Tanya brought to school today was found in this house after we moved in. To me it looked like a plain ceramic plate with some kind of an overglaze.

"I didn't return it to the person who lived here previously because the plate wasn't worth much. Besides, I don't know who lived here before we came. We rented the place through a bank."

All eyes turned on Tanya. She looked at her lap and said nothing.

Papa Lasky shrugged his shoulders. Neither he nor Mama Lasky offered any further explanation. The Bobbseys were baffled.

Finally their host pushed his chair farther from the table and stood up. "Let's see if it's still snowing," he said abruptly.

Was this the man's way of asking the Bobbseys to leave? Following his example, each one at the table carried his dishes to the kitchen.

"It was a super supper," Freddie told Mama Lasky cheerfully.

She spoke coolly and did not smile. "I'm glad you liked it."

Flossie trotted behind her. She was holding two empty glasses, hers and Freddie's. "Is that yummy cake our dessert?" she asked, spying an angel-food cake covered with a creamy white icing.

"It *was*," Mrs. Lasky said.

The little girl lifted her eyes from the delicious dessert. "It *was?*" she repeated, hoping the woman would explain. "You mean we can't have any now?"

Mama Lasky added that the cake had been

baked for angels. "Not for children who like to get into mischief," she observed, "at supper time."

Nan and Bert were within hearing range of her remark. They knew it was meant for Freddie and secretly wished the snow had stopped so they could go home.

Papa Lasky had the same desire. He opened the front door to peer outside. A thick white blanket of snow lay over the ground and street. Snowflakes were falling heavier and faster. As he started to shut the door, a gust of wind blew it back.

He went to the television set and tuned in a local station. An announcer was saying, "Warning! A blizzard is headed this way. Repeat: the weather forecast is for a record fall of snow. Storm warnings are out. The police request that no one drive tonight unless it's an emergency."

The older twins looked at each other in dismay.

CHAPTER IV

BLACKOUT!

"A BLIZZARD!" Freddie and Flossie shouted glee-fully.

"Whoopee!" added the little girl with a giggle.

Papa Lasky groaned. "I suppose you will have to stay here tonight. I couldn't possibly drive you home in this weather."

Bert and Nan did not want to impose on the Laskys any longer but agreed that because of the police warning, they should not leave.

"How wonderful!" Tanya exclaimed. Her face brightened suddenly. "Maybe the snow will keep me in America!"

Flossie, who had ignored Mrs. Lasky's cool

manner, flew to her. "May I have a piece of cake now?" she asked, snuggling against the woman.

Mrs. Lasky could not resist hugging the little girl. "We'll have a snow party!"

"For angels!" exclaimed Flossie.

Bert said he would call their parents to tell them about the change in plans.

"Explain to them," Mrs. Lasky added, "that we will look after you tonight and take you home tomorrow, providing the streets are clear."

Nan walked to the phone with Bert, while Freddie and Flossie went to the dining table for the angel-food cake. Nan could see them whispering to each other. Turning away from them, she took the receiver from Bert and spoke to Mr. and Mrs. Bobbsey. When she faced the dining room again, the younger twins were gone. Mama Lasky was setting out dessert plates with Tanya's help.

"Where are Freddie and Flossie?" Bert inquired.

Mama Lasky, who was now slicing large pieces of the cake, stopped to say, "They are making more magic."

"Uh-oh!" Bert exclaimed. Snapping his fingers, he hurried toward the back door, where the twins' coats and boots had been put to dry. Freddie's and Flossie's were missing!

Nan was behind her brother. He was pulling

on his dampened coat and boots. "Where are you going?" she asked him. "Not into the snow, are you?"

"I certainly am," said Bert. "I'll bet the kids are working their magic outside. The last thing we need right now is a couple of six-year-old snowmen!"

Nan grabbed her coat and slipped it on. A second before she and Bert were ready to go, the back door flew open. Freddie and Flossie stood in front of them.

"Where were you?" Nan quickly asked.

Freddie's red cap was crooked and, like his coat and Flossie's, caked with snow. It had started to melt as soon as they walked into the warm kitchen.

"We brought this," Flossie said, handing over a large paper bag. Inside was a mountain of powdery white snow.

"What are we going to do with that?" Nan asked her sister. "If it stays in here, pretty soon we'll have nothing but a bag full of water!"

Flossie whipped off her coat and boots. "It's a s'prise," she said as Mama Lasky joined the group.

Seeing the wet clothes on hangers and the intriguing bag of snow, she said, "Well, what have my angels been up to?" She bent down.

The little girl cupped her hand over her

mouth and whispered into the woman's ear. Mama Lasky nodded, and the two hurried the others into the dining room.

"Tell Papa and Tanya to come to the table also," were Mrs. Lasky's final words before she went to a kitchen cabinet.

Papa Lasky was still rather quiet when his wife and Flossie reappeared. The woman was holding a tray of small glass bowls.

"I love vanilla ice cream," Tanya said as a dish was placed in front of her.

Happily Flossie announced, "It's not vanilla ice cream. It's snow-scream!"

Thick maple syrup had been poured over the scoop of snow. It made tiny rivers that floated together in the bottom of the bowl. Papa Lasky tasted a spoonful, then quickly dipped in for another one. "Very good," he said.

Bert finished all of his before starting on the cake. "If I ever meet a thief who has a sweet tooth, I'll give him snow-scream with syrup. I'd catch him fast!"

Most of Freddie's dish was empty as well. "You mean," he asked, wiping off a ring of syrup around his lips, " 'cause he'd be too sticky to get away?"

That brought a laugh from everybody, even Tanya, who was already on her second piece of cake.

"Thank you for inviting me to your snow party," she said. "In my country we not do such things."

Freddie wondered why not. "Don't you have snow?" he asked. He thought that must be the reason.

He was surprised when Tanya said, "Oh, we have a lot of snow. Where I come from, in the mountains, sometimes we have a snowfall every day."

"Every day?" interrupted Flossie.

The girl nodded, adding, "But not all year. Just from September through March." She paused a second. "We could have snow parties, lots of them, but my parents would think it is silly. If I go home——" Feeling homesick, she gulped back the rest of her words.

Papa Lasky could not bear to listen to any more. He excused himself and went into the living room. While Bert helped Nan stack the dessert dishes, they could hear the television being switched quickly from one channel to another. Soon he stopped. An announcer whose voice carried above the noise of chatter in the kitchen said he had a special local news report.

"Freddie and I will finish up the chores," Bert said, urging his sisters to join Papa Lasky.

Nan and Flossie were interested to learn that the news bulletin had to do with the Silver Town

Mint Center, where several of their classmates' parents worked. Papa Lasky leaned forward in his chair as if he did not want to miss a word.

The announcer said, "The Silver Town Mint Center, which employs hundreds of Lakeport residents, may have to close its doors at the end of this month."

Flossie whispered to Nan, "Why are the doors open? All the snow could blow inside."

Her sister explained. "He means the company may have to go out of business," Nan said.

Onto the screen flashed the picture of a set of large silver medals glistening in a velvet-lined box. Each disk was engraved with the portrait of a president of the United States.

"Isn't that Mr. Lincoln?" asked Flossie as the TV camera zoomed in on a medal.

"Yes, Floss, Abraham Lincoln, one of our most important presidents," Nan said. "He freed the slaves, but I don't think our present president can help the mint company," she added. "I wish we could, though."

The Silver Town Mint had been accused of sending phony coins and medals to customers! The reporter was now interviewing one of them, a serious-looking woman. "How long have you been buying medals from the mint?" he asked her.

Before answering the question, she noted that she not only bought special medals but also coins. "I even started to collect other things they make," she said, "such as their limited-edition plates."

Nan explained to Flossie what the woman meant by limited edition. "The company makes a bunch of plates with the same design on them. They are sold to people only over a certain amount of time."

Flossie was still a little puzzled. "Then what happens?" she asked.

"Then," Papa Lasky put in, "the designs are destroyed so no more of a particular plate can be sold." He put a finger to his lips, indicating everyone should be quiet.

The woman who was being questioned on television was holding up part of her most recent order from the company. "This is a fake," she said.

Without warning, the television picture faded. The house lights went out, throwing every room into complete darkness. Papa Lasky bolted out of his chair and stumbled against the leg of a table.

"Ow!" he cried, rubbing his knee. "I'll get a flashlight," he said after he recovered from the pain of the blow. He started to feel his way toward the kitchen, when Mama Lasky called out to him.

"The flashlight is dead. I don't think we have any new batteries, unfortunately," she said.

The wind howled against the windowpanes. It sent a shiver through Nan. "Flossie?" she said, but there was no reply. She heard only creaking steps on part of the wooden floor not covered by carpet. "Is that you, Flossie?" she asked again. Still no answer.

Then a sound, much like the wind howling, whistled through the dining room. "Ooh-ooh-ooooooooooh - oooooooooOOOOO - ooooohhhh-shshsh!" The sound grew louder! "I am the snow-ghost!" a voice said in a deep tone that ended in a giggle.

"Freddie Bobbsey!" Nan declared as he pinched Flossie's arm.

The little girl screeched and laughed, then pulled away from her brother. She bounced onto the couch next to Nan. "Boo!" Flossie exclaimed. Her older sister jumped up as Freddie tugged on her hair.

"C'mon, kids," Nan said. "Cool it!" She reached for Freddie's hand, but he was too slippery.

He disappeared into the kitchen again. There was a small screech from Tanya, a few words from Bert, and finally silence. Flossie snuggled up to Nan. "It's so quiet in here," she said. "It's spooky. Where is everybody?"

Nan slipped her arm around the little girl as Mama Lasky, followed by the other children, came into the living room. She held a short burning candle that cast an eerie glow on all their faces. Hers looked worried.

"I am the snow ghost!" a voice said in a deep tone.

"Papa has gone downstairs to check the electric circuit breakers. He thinks they shut off."

"Maybe I ought to see if Papa Lasky needs any help," Bert said when the man did not return shortly.

Letting the light from the candle guide him to the basement door, the boy opened it. He stepped carefully down the stairway into the blackness ahead. Suddenly the cellar and kitchen lights went on.

"Mr. L——" Bert said, but the man was not there.

The door at the end of the room was slightly open. The wind swung it wider. Bert dashed ahead. He called out Papa Lasky's name several times. He tried to see through the heavy curtain of snow falling in front of him.

"Why did Mr. Lasky go out into the storm?" Bert wondered. "Maybe he went to a neighbor's house to see if he could borrow batteries for his flashlight," Bert said to himself, then he cried out, "Papa Lasky, the lights are on!"

Still there was no answer. In the distance, Bert could hear high-pitched bells pealing a strange tune. For a brief moment they stopped playing. Then, as if a hundred bells were rung at the same time, a loud chord of music crashed in the stillness!

CHAPTER V

ICY FIRE

THE weird-sounding bells made Bert shiver almost as much as the icy wind that blew into the basement. Bert realized there was no use calling out to Papa Lasky, so he shut the door.

He dashed upstairs. The other twins and Tanya had entered the kitchen, where Mama Lasky now waited for Bert and her husband to return.

"Where is he?" she asked when Bert reached the landing. She noticed he was alone.

Bert told her about the open basement door and how he had called out in vain.

"We must find Papa!" Her voice became frantic.

"Don't worry," Nan said to Mama Lasky, but her words did not seem to help.

"Something may happen to him!" Mama cried out in panic.

The younger twins drew closer to her. Tanya spoke up. "Mama, please tell me what is wrong."

But her mother would not reveal what was troubling her. She gazed at Bert, a plea in her eyes. Without wasting a minute, he and Freddie grabbed their coats and boots. "We'll find Papa Lasky," they said.

Though Mama was deeply worried about her husband, she said, "But maybe you should wait until the snow stops. I don't want you to catch cold."

Nan knew the storm would not keep her brothers from going on their search. "Don't stay out too long," she told them. "Bert, will you do something for me?" She fished into the pocket of her coat, which had hung next to Bert's.

"Okay," he said. "What is it?"

She handed him the woolen cap he had refused to wear earlier. Nan said, "Please put this on."

With a sigh, he gave in to his twin's request. Then he and Freddie scurried down the cellar steps and out through the basement door. The wind was still blowing hard, whipping the snow into high drifts. Whatever footprints Papa Lasky had made were completely covered now.

"I can't see anything," Freddie said. He squinted against the snowflakes.

Bert was glad to wear the warm cap. "Stick close to me," he called out to his brother.

Freddie pulled up his collar, pinching it close around his neck. He mumbled into his coat, as he and Bert battled through the storm. They noticed that the houses and street lamps across the road were dark, while all those on the Lasky side were on.

"The whole area must have had a blackout," Bert announced to Freddie, who sank his face deeper into his coat.

The older boy called out Papa Lasky's name. Then Freddie, whose teeth were chattering, joined in. But the only reply was the steady scraping of branches.

"Let's go home, Bert," begged the little boy. He pulled his wool cap down as far as it would stretch. "I'm c-c-cold."

They had walked more than half a block. Bert tried to figure out why Lasky had left the house. The boy detective glanced at the frame house nearest the Lasky's, where the man probably would have gone for help. There was not a single light on and no evidence that anyone was home. Ideas swirled in Bert's brain.

"Maybe Papa Lasky didn't go out for batteries," he concluded. "He's mysterious. Something big must be wrong. Mama Lasky wouldn't say. Does Tanya know?"

Deep in thought, Bert had not paid attention to Freddie's plea. "Are you with me?" he asked, turning back to look for his brother.

A few feet behind him Freddie was slipping and sliding through the snow. He had tried to keep pace with Bert, but the numbness of his feet had slowed him down. Now he hurried forward to meet Bert, who was at the corner.

"I'm c-c-coming," Freddie said.

Seconds later they started to cross the street. Suddenly headlight beams threw the shadows of the pair across the snow. They turned to discover a small truck whipping toward them.

"Freddie, watch out!" Bert screamed as the van cut through the snow at reckless speed.

In a flash the older boy grabbed his brother and pulled him out of the way. They slid on a crust of ice and plunged into the snowbank at the curb. The vehicle hurried past, missing the brothers by a few inches.

As Freddie struggled to sit up, Bert remained perfectly still. He kept a sharp eye on the truck, making a mental note of the license plate. It was WCK-250. The picture of a bell had been painted on the back door.

Thinking of others he had seen on similar vans in Lakeport, Bert said to himself, "Maybe it's a

"Freddie, watch out!" Bert screamed.

telephone truck, except it doesn't have a ladder on top."

Freddie made a feeble attempt to stand up. But snowflakes were now mixed with a fine icy drizzle that created a slippery glaze on the ground. The little boy fell into the snowbank.

"Oops!" he cried.

This time he landed on his back, and lay spread-eagled on the street. He did not make any effort to move. Bert scrambled to his brother's side.

"Did you hurt yourself?" he asked.

Shaking his head, Freddie swung his weight to one side but could not get a firm grip on the quickly forming ice. Bert, however, managed to get up.

"Here, take my hand," he said, reaching out.

The little boy quickly did as Bert suggested but Freddie could not get up. Bert moved backward, hoping Freddie could get a foothold somehow. Instead, Bert lost his balance and was dragged down again.

Although they were miserably cold, both boys burst into laughter. "Now what'll we do?" Bert asked. "We'll soon turn into icicles!"

"Or freezicles-cles!" Freddie added with a shiver.

The wind was still blowing strongly as Bert once again stumbled to his feet. He grabbed Freddie's arms and pulled him up. Together, this time linking arms, the two Bobbseys safely crossed to the next corner.

"Can't we go back?" Freddie pleaded, as they headed in the opposite direction.

Bert's answer was short. "Soon."

It seemed to the little boy that hours had gone by. The hard-falling sleet stung his face and flattened the peak of his cap.

In the distance the bells Bert had listened to earlier were pealing their eerie melody. This time they sounded farther away. "Was it because of the shifting wind?" the boy detective wondered.

Bert did not take long to think about a possible answer. Ahead, a man was staggering slowly through the snow. Bert tried to walk faster but he and Freddie were held back by the storm.

"Papa Lasky!" Freddie exclaimed when he recognized the stocky form.

The man did not respond. He seemed to be swaying. One arm was across his forehead to shield his face from the wind.

"Papa Lasky!" Bert called out. "It's Bert and Freddie Bobbsey!"

The shouts seemed to go unheard. A couple of times the boys slid on the ice but did not fall. They drew closer to the man.

"I think he's been wandering around out here a long time," Bert said to Freddie. Sleet had caked itself on Papa Lasky's clothing. He seemed to be confused about which way to go.

Suddenly the street lamps across the road went on. As the boys glanced up at them, they noticed that there was a lot of thickening ice on the long black wires strung between trees. Suddenly one snapped, then another.

Papa Lasky halted as the power lines slipped down through a tree near him and circled close to his body. Sparks flew in all directions.

"Oh no!" Bert cried out, watching ice-covered tree limbs break off and crash behind the man.

They brought more of the dangerous, sparking wires down, completely blocking Papa Lasky's escape. By instinct he tried to back away from the sizzling power lines.

But he was trapped. Fear spread over his face. His cry for help was choked by the wind. Helpless, he stared at the boys, who now stood within a few feet of him.

"Papa Lasky, don't move!" Bert exclaimed.

CHAPTER VI

GHOSTLY MELODY

BERT's warning sent a quiver through Papa Lasky. Nervously he watched the sparking wires. They had curled themselves into a small circle around him. He could not take more than two or three steps without touching one.

"Maybe I can take a chance and try to hop over them," he said.

"No, don't!" Bert cried. "The power company will turn off the current in a minute or two. Right now it's so icy you might slip when you jump."

"And b-be 'lectricicuted," added Freddie. Bert knew his small brother was trying to say, "Electrocuted."

"I guess you're right," Papa Lasky agreed.

It was evident that he was exhausted. He was short of breath and his face, wet from the sleet, looked pale and tired. "Call the police," he directed Bert. "The current isn't off yet, and who knows when it will be?"

Just then a woman in the neighboring house came to the door. "Do you have a couple of old rubber tires?" Bert asked her.

Before she could reply, Papa Lasky spoke. "This is no time to play games!" he bellowed with all of his strength. "Call the police!"

Freddie knew the man was upset. But he did not like to hear such a remark made about his brother. Bert would never play games when somebody was in trouble! "My brother is trying to help you!" the little boy yelled.

Papa Lasky's face, which had been very pale, now reddened. He took a step forward. A spark flew up in front of him. It frightened the trapped man. He stepped back.

"Mommy told me and Flossie we should never touch the 'lectric stove or the toaster or the iron when they're on," put in Freddie, " 'cause we might get a shock. You better not touch those wires."

In the meantime Bert was trying to get an answer to his question and started up the front walk to the house. The woman had not heard him clearly the first time. Her husband came to the door to see what was the matter. Through the thickly falling snow and sleet they could barely detect the fallen wires, now white like broken tree branches.

"Why are you wandering around in this kind of weather?" the young man asked Bert.

As quickly as Bert could, he explained what had happened. When he mentioned Papa Lasky's name to the couple, they stiffened. The man drew back from the door.

"I'm sorry," he said. "I can't help Mr. Lasky. Let the power company do it. I'll phone them."

Bert was stunned. "But Mr. Lasky's in bad shape and ought to go right home," he said.

The man's wife tugged his arm. "He needs you," she said. "Don't hold a grudge against him."

Her husband did not give in at first.

"And how is he going to help us when I'm out of work?" he asked.

Bert wondered what the man was talking about. How was Papa Lasky responsible for this man's job? But more important than finding out was rescuing Papa Lasky. "Please, sir," Bert begged.

The numbness began to leave his face as he felt the warm air of the hallway. Although only a few seconds passed before the man made up his mind, it seemed forever to Bert.

Looking out at the snow, he sighed. "Okay. I'll meet you down by the garage. My name's Rankin."

His decision brought a smile from his wife. Bert nodded. He glanced toward Papa Lasky and Freddie. With careful steps he worked his way to the garage door, which the young man opened from inside. Along the wall were some old tires.

"Are you related to the Laskys?" Mr. Rankin asked Bert. He rolled one of the tires to the boy.

"No," Bert replied. "I go to school with Tanya."

Without making any further comment about the Laskys, the young man said, "Take the tire down the driveway. I'll roll the other one."

He and the boy skidded as they rolled the tires slowly to the street. Rankin told Bert and Freddie to stand back while he flung the first tire on top of the electric wires, then the second one next to it.

"Step on the tires," Bert said to Papa Lasky.

Freddie peered out through a buttonhole of his heavy jacket. "Won't he get a shock?" he asked his brother.

"He'll be okay," Bert answered. "Electricity won't pass through rubber."

The older boy reached toward the man, motioning him to take his hand. Shakily, Papa Lasky edged forward. The neighbor took his other hand.

"Step on the tires!" Bert said.

Even though he had to walk only a few steps, it was difficult for him. He mounted the tires slowly.

"I'm going to fall," he said. The soles of his boots were icy and slipped on the tires.

But Mr. Rankin managed to pull him firmly across.

"Oh, thank you, thank you," he said, still shaking from his ordeal. He looked at his neighbor, whose stern expression had not changed a bit.

"It was his idea to use the tires," Mr. Rankin said. "He's a smart kid." Turning to Bert, he added, "I'll bet you could solve almost any problem. I wish you could save Silver Town Mint."

Papa Lasky winced at the remark but did not say anything. Without a good-by or "I'm glad you weren't hurt," Mr. Rankin dragged the tires off the power lines. With Bert's help, he rolled them back to the garage.

"Why don't you like Papa Lasky?" Bert asked him.

The reply was a pat on the shoulder. "I used to admire his work a great deal," he said. "You'd better run home now and get out of those wet clothes."

Bert left but on the way back to the Lasky's, he wondered, "Why wouldn't he explain? Something terrible must have happened between them."

He tried to piece together the few bits of conversation he had heard between the Rankins, and the strange comment Mr. Rankin had made to Bert about helping Silver Town Mint. How could Papa Lasky be mixed up with the trouble there?

By the time Bert caught up to Freddie and Papa Lasky, the two were huddling together for warmth. The wind had died down a little but the sting of its chill could still be felt.

The man put one arm across Bert's shoulder. "You saved me. I really don't know how to thank you," he said.

The peal of bells in the distance stopped Bert from replying right away. "Papa Lasky," he said, after the mysterious melody ended, "do you know anything about those weird bells?"

Freddie added, "They sound funny."

Papa Lasky took a longer stride through the deep snow toward his home. "Those aren't real bells playing," he said. "It's the carillon on the second floor of the Silver Town Mint Museum."

Freddie had never heard the word before. "What's a car-on? You mean like a motor running?" he asked.

Eyes twinkling, Papa Lasky replied, "No, my little friend, not like a motor running. A carillon is a big music box that makes beautiful bell sounds. Did you ever see the gongs in a grandfather clock? The gongs in a carillon sound like bells. When they are hit with a metal hammer they make beautiful music."

Bert quickly pointed out that the bells they
had heard were not beautiful.

"The electric machinery that starts the bells
playing has been acting up lately, so the music
isn't beautiful. Besides, it's off schedule and plays
at odd times," the stocky man said.

Freddie seemed confused. "I never saw a music
box that had a clock," he said.

Papa Lasky slowed his pace as the wind rose
again. "The carillon does have a timer on it," he
said. "You're pretty smart to have figured that
out. I didn't tell you anything about a clock."

The nice remark made Freddie forget that he
was cold. "When does the music box play?" he
asked.

The man's answer gave a clue to something
more about himself. "Morning, noon, and quit-
ting time," he said.

Bert asked, "Then you work at the Silver
Town Mint?"

He could feel the muscles in the man's arm
tighten. "I used to," Papa Lasky said.

"Didn't you like it there?" Freddie asked.

Papa Lasky did not reply. The trio had finally
reached his house. "How did you know where to
look for me?" he asked.

Freddie said, "You left the basement door
open."

Bert added, "I thought maybe you went to a
neighbor's to borrow batteries or a flashlight. We

knew you couldn't go far in the storm on foot and we didn't hear your car start up."

The man seemed amazed by Bert's answer. "I'm beginning to believe you really are detectives," he said.

The boys stamped their feet on the landing of the front steps while Papa Lasky opened the door. Secretly Bert and Freddie were thrilled to think that they had finally proven themselves to be detectives!

Mysteriously Papa Lasky added, "I didn't go out into the storm to borrow a flashlight." He paused.

Was he ready to confide in them? the boys wondered.

"We can talk about it tomorrow," he promised, as they stepped out of the cold night and into the cozy house.

CHAPTER VII

FLOSSIE'S BRAVERY

THE warmth of the Lasky home felt so good!

"I'm cold through to my bones!" Freddie declared.

Papa Lasky collapsed into a big chair in front of the fireplace. He did not wait to take off his snow-covered coat and boots.

"Papa!" Tanya exclaimed joyfully, running into the living room. "Where have you been? We were so worried about you."

Mama Lasky had made hot chocolate and was carrying in a large china pot of it on a tray. When she saw her husband and the boys, she quickly put down the tray and hurried to Papa Lasky.

"Are you all right? You must get out of these

wet clothes," she said to him. "You too," she added with a glance at Bert and Freddie, who were standing next to him.

The boys went to the kitchen to hang their coats where they would dry fast. Nan and Flossie were gathering a pile of napkins and cups and saucers onto a tray.

"Oh goodie, you're home!" cried Flossie. "Where'd you find Papa Lasky?"

"On some electric wires," Bert said, grinning.

Flossie frowned, puzzled, but Nan said, "Come on, give it to us straight."

As soon as the boys had hung up their coats and dried their wet hair a bit, Bert explained what had happened. The girls were amazed.

"It sounds," said Nan, "as if the Silver Town Mint Center has more than one mystery! I wonder what Papa Lasky wants to tell you."

Later that night, after they had gone to bed, Nan and Flossie heard a low whimper coming from Tanya's bed across the room. Was she crying? Nan raised herself from the cot she had been sleeping on to look at the girl.

Flossie whispered to her sister, "What's the matter with Tanya?"

The girl, hearing her name, sat up. She wiped her eyes. In the light of the full moon Nan could see tears streaming down her friend's face. Yawning, Flossie got out of bed and curled up against Tanya.

"You can tell us what's the matter," she said sweetly. This made Tanya smile a little.

Nan propped her pillow under her head and asked, "Are you worried about going back to your country?"

The girl shook her head. "No. If I have to go, I will."

The twins were surprised by her answer. "Are you 'fraid of all the snow?" Flossie said, trying to think of a reason.

Again Tanya said she was not, but she added, "I heard Mama and Papa talking about some trouble he is in. People believe he stole something. I was afraid it was the plate from the museum."

The Bobbseys wanted to know more of the details. "Who thinks he stole something?" Flossie asked.

Tanya slipped under the covers and Flossie went back to her bed. "Where he worked," Tanya said. "But he didn't do anything wrong. He couldn't. He's too nice."

Nan thought, "I wonder if he might have been involved in the trouble at the mint." Aloud she asked, "Did you hear them say anything else?"

Tanya said she had told Nan and Flossie everything. "You are detectives. You can help him," she said. "Please."

"We'll try," Flossie answered, dozing off again.

A creaking sound above made her open her eyes wide.

"What's that?" Nan asked.

The three girls listened carefully as the sound repeated itself. "Someone's in the attic," declared Tanya quietly.

Flossie was eager to find out who it was. "Let's go up!" she exclaimed.

But Tanya pulled the sheet up around her neck. "Oh no, we stay here. No one is allowed to go there."

That did not seem to bother the younger Bobbsey at all. "If there's an 'intooter' in the house, we've got to get him!" she said.

Nan kept out of the discussion for a moment. Tanya replied, "Maybe it is Papa. He works there sometimes."

This remark did not slip past the older twin. "It's pretty early to be working," she said. "Does Papa Lasky do this often?"

She stared out the window at the blanket of snow, covered by a silvery glaze that stretched across the front yard. Nan waited for an answer.

After a long pause, Tanya said, "Not often."

The twins pulled themselves out of their cots and put on robes borrowed from Tanya. "C'mon," Flossie said to her.

Soon they began their slow climb up the stairway that led to the third-floor storage room. It was the one Tanya claimed was Papa Lasky's workshop. Tiptoing in single file, the girls reached a door at the top. It might squeak when they opened it.

Nan glanced at Flossie and their friend for a vote. Tanya replied in a whisper, "Let's go back!"

But Flossie was not going to give up easily. "We're here now. Don't worry, Tanya."

Nan turned the knob carefully. At first the door would not budge. Then it swung free without making a sound. The moon shining through a bare window cast a glow on a metal table and various tools. The rest of the room was pitch-black.

A twinge of fear went through Tanya as she looked around. A gasp from Flossie startled the other two.

"Oh-oh!" she said, pointing to a box that had slid away from another one in the corner. The space between them revealed the edge of a long yellow gown. The little girl scuffed toward a thick roll of paper that poked out of a wastebasket. Nan tugged her back but Flossie pulled away. She picked up the paper. With slow, quiet strides she headed for the yellow gown. Taking a big fearless leap, she rushed upon it.

"Got you!" the little girl exclaimed and with all her strength, which was not very great, she hit the bent-over figure on the back of his head with the roll of paper.

"Ow!" It was Freddie! "What did you do that for?" he asked, looking straight at his twin.

"I-I-I——" was all the little girl could say as he stood up to his full height.

He reached for the paper roll and knocked over a tower of small boxes. "Boy, did you goof!" he exclaimed.

Tanya, who had frozen into complete silence, now screeched. "We're going to get into a lot of trouble," she said.

Nan put a comforting hand on the girl's shoulder. "Freddie," she called in a whisper.

The little boy stepped into view. He was wearing Papa Lasky's extra large and extra long nightshirt. On his head was an oversized nightcap. Even Tanya could not help laughing.

"You look like a yellow Santa Claus!" she said.

Nan gazed at Freddie. "What are you doing up here?"

The little boy stumbled over his trailing gown and kicked one of the boxes out of his way.

"Sh!" said Nan. "We don't want to wake up the others."

Freddie drew closer to the girls. "I just wanted to look around here."

"What for?" Flossie asked.

" 'Cause," was his vague reply.

" 'Cause why?" his twin returned. "You're a big snoop, Freddie Bobbsey!"

Her brother frowned. "I am not."

It was Freddie!

"You are too!" she said.

"Am not."

The argument might have gone on for some time, but Nan stopped it. "You still haven't told us what you were looking for at this hour."

The little boy said he wanted to investigate the attic. "Isn't this where you found that plate?" he asked Tanya.

She nodded.

"I thought maybe I could find a clue to the person who left it here," he went on, "or even find the other plate."

Nan and Flossie were amazed. "What other plate?" they asked together.

"Well, Tanya's was a copy of another one. Right?" he responded. "Copied from the museum plate."

His sisters reminded him that the copy could have been modeled after a photograph.

"I don't think so," the young detective said.

"Why not?" Nan and Flossie wanted to know.

"It's just a hunch," he said, yawning. "I want to go to sleep now."

But Tanya had grown interested in the conversation. "What did you find out?" she asked. "Did you solve the mystery?"

The little boy stretched his arms high and yawned again.

"Well?" Nan asked. "We'd like to hear all about your clue."

Freddie pulled the nightcap over his eyes, then down to his neck. He muffled his words into the soft material. With a quick tug his twin yanked it off his head, ruffling his curls.

"I didn't find anything," said Freddie, "but I only went through one box. I have to look in all the others. Want to help?" he asked with a mischievous twinkle in his eyes.

Nan could not believe her ears. "Certainly not and you won't either. It's not nice to go poking through other people's things," she declared.

The little boy said that wasn't what he was doing. "I was invester-ating," he said, taking his cap from Flossie. He tripped forward.

The girls laughed but became somber when heavy footsteps echoed below.

"That must be Papa! What if he finds us here?" Tanya asked.

The footsteps reached the bottom landing of the stairway and started to climb slowly. Quickly Nan shut the door as Flossie and Freddie scurried to a hiding place behind the boxes. The older twin crept quietly out of the moonbeams that shone on her and knelt under the metal table. Frantic, Tanya could not find a box large enough to shield her from view.

The footsteps drew nearer. Tanya flattened herself against the wall. She held her breath, waiting for the person on the other side of the door to open it.

He paused a long moment, then took a few steps down as if he had changed his mind. None of the children stirred. Perhaps they could go back to bed without anyone else knowing about Freddie's mischief.

Then the footsteps started upward again. The doorknob turned.

CHAPTER VIII

M-Y-S-T-E-R-Y

As THE doorknob turned, the children held their breaths. Once again the door swung open. It bounced gently against Tanya and finally came to rest. She did not make the slightest move, keeping her hands and arms stretched as flat as possible on the wall behind her.

The heavy shadow of Papa Lasky in robe and slippers loomed large in the moonlight. He went to the metal worktable, but did not see Nan crouching beneath it.

"Anybody up here?" he boomed. His strong voice sent shivers through his listeners.

How would they explain what they were doing in his workroom? Nan's knees ached from her awkward position. She wanted to stand up or sprawl, do anything to relieve the stiffness in her legs. But she did not dare move. Instead she watched the man's broad feet turn, take a few steps, then turn again.

"Humph!" he said to himself, walking to one end of the room, away from Freddie and Flossie's hiding place.

Tanya slowly turned her head. Her eyes followed the man as he pulled on a chain lamp that hung in the corner. It lit up dimly.

"Oh, he will find us for sure," she thought.

To her surprise Papa Lasky merely pushed a few boxes aside, then reached for the chain again and shut off the light. He hummed softly as he returned to the center of the room. Giving the place one more sweeping glance, he put his hand on the doorknob.

"How wonderful!" Tanya thought.

Nan too wanted to jump for joy. The younger twins, however, had not been able to watch the man's movements. Freddie pinched his nose, trying to hold back a sneeze. When he thought it had passed, he let go. But the feeling came back. He could not stop it.

"Achoo! Achoo! Achoo!" He sneezed loudly.

In reply Papa Lasky said, "God bless you!"

Sheepishly the children came out of their hiding places. Freddie's nightcap was pulled low over his face.

"You can't hide from me." The big man laughed and took the cap off the little boy.

He sneezed again. "I didn't mean to do it," Freddie said. "Really I didn't."

Papa Lasky asked the four to sit down. They hopped up on the long table. "If you didn't mean to do it, then why did you do it?" he asked Freddie. "And what did you do?"

"Nothing," was the young twin's reply.

The children were amazed that the man did not seem to be angry. "Well, if you did nothing, then why did you say you didn't mean to do it?"

The question stumped the little detective. His sister Flossie spoke up instead. "I'm sorry, Papa Lasky."

One after the other Nan and Tanya said they were wrong to have come to the attic without asking permission. Seeing that their remarks had aroused Papa Lasky's curiosity, Nan decided to explain fully.

"We thought there was an intruder in the house. It turned out to be my little brother," she said.

Freddie dangled his feet over the table and told his story. He mumbled part of it as he went along. Papa Lasky did not hear it all but did not ask Freddie to speak up or repeat any of it.

"You children astound me," the man said when the boy finished talking. "I have never known any children who want to solve mysteries as much as you do."

He hugged each of them, saying, "You saved me once. Maybe, just maybe, you can do it again!"

Nan wished that Bert were awake to hear all this. The moon still cast its bright glow on the room. It made the whole incident seem unreal to the older Bobbsey girl. She wondered, Was Papa Lasky going to reveal his story to them now?

He looked at the younger twins, whose eyelids were drooping. "You all go back to sleep," he said kindly. "In the morning, when we are wide awake, I will tell you *my* mystery."

His last word made Freddie and Flossie sit up. "Ooh, what is it?" the little girl asked. Without asking again, she yawned and stretched her arms toward the fatherly man.

Carefully he lifted her and told the others to be very quiet as they went downstairs. "We don't want to wake up Mama," he said, "or Bert."

Saying good night to Nan and Tanya, he tucked Flossie in her cot. Tanya drifted to sleep quickly but Nan lay staring at the ceiling. The Bobbseys had never met anyone quite like Papa Lasky. His behavior, which changed like the wind itself, puzzled Nan.

Over and over she recounted the events of their stay. Mr. Lasky had thrown the silver-bell plate clear across the living room. Yet now, when Freddie explained why he had gone to the attic, it did not seem to disturb the man. Would he change his mind and not tell the twins what was troubling him?

Nan knew it was senseless to worry. She would have her answer soon enough. She turned on her side and went to sleep.

In a few hours sunlight was streaming through the window of Tanya's room. Nan buried her head in the pillow to block out the brightness. Then she rolled over and squinted at the other beds. The covers on each one were heaped up like two humps on a camel's back. Flossie and Tanya were already up! Nan looked at the clock on the dresser. It was eight o'clock!

She glanced out the window. A huge plow truck was pushing snow against the street curb.

From downstairs came a loud announcement over the radio. "All schools in Lakeport closed today!"

Freddie cried out, "Wah-hoo!"

"Bee-yoo-ti-ful!" said Flossie.

When Nan arrived at the breakfast table, the younger twins teased her. "Here comes sleepy-head!" Flossie exclaimed.

Mama Lasky said cheerfully, "It was your mid-night adventure that kept you awake." Apparently she had already heard about the episode in the attic.

Nan smiled. "Bert, you missed a lot," she told him.

Her twin grinned. "Yes, worse luck."

Mama Lasky placed bowls of cereal in front of the children. Flossie looked closely at hers before pouring milk on top of it.

"It's an alphabet cereal!" the little girl exclaimed. Gleefully she spread her napkin next to the bowl.

Dipping her tiny fingers in, she pulled out a few of the crunchy letters. "I have a message for you," she said to Papa Lasky, who was sipping orange juice.

He raised his bushy eyebrows, waiting for the child to spell it out. "M-Y-S-T-E-R-Y," she said.

All the children laughed, including Flossie, who put the letters back in her bowl and ate them.

"You are so clever, Flossie," Tanya said, glancing at her American father.

"I get your message, dear," Papa Lasky answered. "I promised you I would tell my mystery story and I will. As you heard on the television last night the Silver Town Mint Center is in big trouble. So am I. You see, I——" It was difficult for the man to continue.

Bert said, "If you would rather not talk about it, that's all right."

But Papa Lasky waved his hand as if to say, "Don't worry about me."

"M-Y-S-T-E-R-Y," Flossie said.

He went on without pausing again. "I was an engraver for the mint. That is, I carve pictures or designs onto steel plates called dies. Artists draw the pictures or designs for me to copy.

"Recently many pictures and dies have been stolen from the company. I have been accused of stealing them!"

"How dreadful!" said Nan.

Papa Lasky went on, "The thief is using the drawings and the dies to make cheap phony imitations of our silver pieces. What's even worse, the thief somehow got hold of the mint's list of customers who collect coins and medals and other special things. The thief has already delivered pieces and received money for them—much more money than they're worth."

Bert asked, "Why does the company think you stole the designs and drawings?"

Papa Lasky explained that the Silver Town Mint had security guards throughout the plant. "Supposedly I was the last person to work with the drawings before they disappeared."

Nan had not missed a word of what Papa Lasky had been saying. She asked, "Do you think it might have been an inside job by somebody else?"

"Most likely," he replied. "Anyway, I've been fired!"

Tanya rushed to his side, putting her arms around him. "Oh, Papa, that is why I must go home," she said in despair.

"I am afraid so," Mama Lasky spoke up.

The Bobbseys were upset. An innocent man had been accused and then lost his job!

Freddie doubled up his fists. "If we ever find that bad man, I'll——I'll——"

"I know," said Flossie. "You'll turn your fire engine hose on him!"

Bert asked, "Papa Lasky, did your walk in the snow last night have something to do with all this?"

Papa Lasky nodded. "When I heard the news report on TV last night, I became frantic. As you have seen, I am very nervous and lose control of my temper when I don't mean to.

"I decided to see a neighbor who also works for the Silver Town Mint. I wanted to talk with him about the situation. But when I reached his house, it was dark. I did not realize there had been a blackout in the area. It was not the time for a visit so I started back. You know the rest."

Bert thought of the other neighbor, who had half-heartedly helped him and Freddie rescue the man. "Do a lot of employees of the company live around here?" he asked.

"Yes," Mr. Lasky said. "And they are not very friendly to me and my wife. They think I am guilty of taking the designs and drawings." His voice rose. "I would never do such a thing. I am an engraver, not a thief. The company is losing customers rapidly. Everybody is blaming me."

"Please finish your breakfast," his wife said kindly.

When they were done eating, Bert suggested something that immediately appealed to his brother and sisters. "Since school is closed, maybe we could visit the Silver Town Mint."

Nan smiled. "That's a super idea. We can hunt for clues to help Papa Lasky."

The engraver said he was not allowed to enter the buildings but would drive the children to the door. Excited, the twins called home to make sure it was all right for them to go. Mrs. Bobbsey answered the phone.

When she heard what her children wanted to do, she said, "I wish I could go with you. I'm very interested in the medals the mint makes. But I'm afraid the driveway is still packed with snow. Your father and Sam are outside cleaning it, but I don't think we'll be taking the car anywhere for a while."

Sam was the kindly, smiling man who had worked in Mr. Bobbsey's lumberyard for years. He and his wife Dinah lived on the third floor of the twins' home.

In less than an hour the Bobbseys were on their way. They had tried to convince Tanya to go along, but she said she would stay at home and help Mama Lasky with chores.

A long winding driveway led to the Silver Town Mint Center. Sprawled across the snow-

covered terrace were two modern white buildings. One was the firm's museum and the other,
its factory. Papa Lasky pulled into the visitors'
parking area and let the children out.

"I'll pick you up at noontime." he said and
pointed to a sign on which was printed: MAIN
ENTRANCE TO FACTORY.

The children waved good-by and went inside.
A young woman greeted them, saying, "I'm Miss
Arnold. You'd like a trip through the mint?"

"Yes, thank you," Bert said.

In a short while a guide led them to a room
that contained big machines. Sheets of silver were
being fed through it. As the metal rolled along,
towering pipes moved up and down. They
punched out small round pieces of the silver.

"That sure is a big cookie cutter!" Flossie exclaimed, watching the silver blanks pour into a
large cart.

"You could break a tooth on those cookies,"
the guide said with a smile. "This is the first step
in minting a silver coin or a medal."

She introduced the twins to Michael, one of
the workers, adding that he would look after
them. As he started to lead the children around
the giant machine, the phone rang. To the twins'
surprise, most of the other workmen, who had
been busy pushing carts of silver blanks to another section, disappeared.

Suddenly there was a rumble of wheels and a shout from Michael. "Watch out!" he cried. "Run!"

Instantly he shinned up a pole, signaling to the children to hurry. Bert saw a flash of curly red hair as two giant carts loaded with silver blanks rolled at full speed toward the Bobbseys!

CHAPTER IX

FALSE ALARM!

As THE giant carts of silver rumbled toward the Bobbseys, the four detectives scattered. Bert shinned up the pole after Michael. Nan and the young twins darted around the cutting machine just as the carts crashed into each other. They barely missed the children. One cart toppled over. Hundreds of silver disks poured onto the floor and swept Freddie and Flossie off their feet.

"Oopty-doo!" Flossie cried, as she landed in a heap of silver.

Her older sister skidded, tripped, then fell too. "Ouch!" she exclaimed, glancing up at the bank of windows along the top of one wall.

For a moment she forgot about the edges of silver pieces that grazed against her legs. A man with curly red hair was leering down at the twins. When his eyes met Nan's, he pulled away.

The others had not noticed the mysterious on-looker. To them Nan seemed to be in a daze. "Are you okay?" Bert called out to her, and slid down the pole. Michael was behind him.

The older girl winced a bit as she stood up. "Sure," she said. "What about Freddie and Flossie?"

The young twins had already recovered from the frightening experience. Flossie grinned at Freddie, who lay stretched out on the floor. Silver disks were sprinkled over him. Flossie put pieces of silver on his eyes and mouth.

"Freddie's a silver silly!" she exclaimed. She tried to spin another piece on his nose. "Spinny-boom!" Flossie giggled, as the silver disk fell to the floor.

"Are you sure you're not hurt?" Michael asked.

"Mm-huh," Freddie replied. He shook his head and sat up. Most of the silver pieces slid off his clothes.

His twin stopped playing too. "I'm okay," she said.

The workman looked angry. "Who shoved that cart at us?" he asked.

"Some meanie!" Flossie replied.

By now the workers who had mysteriously left the room had come back. "Hey, what's going on here?" one of the men asked. They stared at the overturned cart and silver strewn over the floor.

"I told you they ought not to let kids run loose in the plant!" a scruffy-faced man bellowed.

"Yeah, that's right!" a few others joined in.

The Bobbseys waited until the men quieted down before explaining. "You see," Bert started to say, but he was interrupted.

"You've got it all wrong," Michael told the men. "Somebody deliberately tried to run us down with these bulldogs!"

Flossie tugged on his dark-green shirt. "I don't see any bulldogs," she said.

"I don't either!" roared one of the men.

Ignoring the remark, Michael answered the little girl. "That's what I call these carts."

Freddie was trying to figure out the reason. "R-R-ruff-r-ruff!" he barked at the still-turning rollers on the bulldog that lay upside down.

A few of the men chuckled at the boy but became serious again. They let Michael finish his story. When he was done, the scruffy-faced man declared, "That's the craziest thing I've ever heard!"

"No, it isn't," Nan spoke up. She looked around, hoping to spot the curly red hair that had flashed in and out of view behind the windows.

One had strawberry-blond hair but it was rather straight.

Just then a security guard arrived. "I saw the whole thing on our closed-circuit TV," he announced.

"Then you know who did it?" Nan asked him, excited.

The guard smiled kindly. "Unfortunately part of the picture fuzzed up so I couldn't see what caused the carts to start rolling. It happened so fast—I had my eyes only on you kids," he said. "Say, aren't you the famous Bobbsey twins?"

"I don't know how famous we are," Nan said modestly.

"But we're detectives!" Freddie piped up.

"I know," the guard said. "You're pretty popular in Lakeport. I've seen your pictures in the paper with stories about the mysteries you solved."

The other men shifted uneasily. The scruffy-faced man mumbled, "I'm sorry. I didn't know who you were. We get some brats here. Do you know what I mean?"

Bert nodded. He wondered whether Danny Rugg had ever visited the Silver Town Mint. "Would you mind if I ask you something?"

"Go ahead," the guard said.

"Why did all of you leave this room after the phone rang?" was Bert's first question.

One of the men volunteered to answer it. "We were called to a meeting."

"Who requested it?"

"Our floor supervisor. But when we got to the room where it was supposed to be held, nobody was there."

Another man added quickly, "The floor super said he didn't want to see us."

Bert suspected the call was a hoax. "Somebody got you out of here in a hurry so he could scare us!"

Freddie added, "That's right. And maybe it had something to do with another mystery we're working on. We want to help Tanya and Papa and Mama Lasky."

The name Lasky made some of the men bristle angrily. Bert nudged his brother to stop talking. "Could we see some of the other rooms?" he asked Michael.

"Yes," Flossie said. "I want to see where Papa Las——"

Nan squeezed her sister's shoulder as a signal to stop.

Michael escorted the children to another area, which was marked "Engraving Room." It was smaller than the cutting room and painted the same cold white. Lined up in the center, like a row of soldiers, were ten gray metal desks. A man sat behind each one. All of them were peering through small magnifying glasses at pieces of steel. They were no larger than fat thumbs.

"What are they doing?" Flossie asked.

One of the engravers came forward. After exchanging a few words with Michael, the man shook hands with each twin.

Michael said, "I'm sorry I have to leave you children, but I must get back to my post. Mr. Wilson will take good care of you. Hope I bump into you again," he added with a twinkle in his eyes, "but I hope nothing else does!"

The twins grinned too. Nan thanked him for helping them, then the Bobbseys went to Mr. Wilson's chair and stood behind him. He let Flossie look through his magnifying glass.

"What do you see?" he asked her.

"It looks like a soldier. He has a baby in his arms," she said. "There's something written all around the picture. Nan, you read it."

Her sister took Flossie's place. She was amazed by the fine details carved into the metal piece. There was a slight smile on the soldier's face.

"He looks so alive, as if he's running toward us."

"What does it say, sis?" Flossie prodded.

The tiny letters swept in a half-circle at the top of the picture. "It says, 'Flight to Freedom.'" Nan could not take her eyes off the piece. "It's lovely."

"It says, 'Flight to Freedom,'" Nan said.

Mr. Wilson, a shy man, blushed. "It will be lovelier when every step is finished and a silver medal is made. This is a steel hub. It is only a model for a die."

Bert had read a little about the minting process and said, "The die is just the reverse of the hub. It's the design turned inside out, isn't it?"

"Umm, I prefer to say the design turned outside in. Right now I am checking the hub to make sure every detail of the original design is there. If an extra strand of hair is needed, I put it in. If the baby's tear is missing, I carve that in. Then the hub will be pressed into a softened cone of steel. Hundreds of thousands of pounds of pressure will be used to force this image into the face of the die."

Flossie's and Freddie's eyes popped wide open. "As heavy as those big carts that hold the silver blanks?" the little boy asked.

The engraver frowned. "Oh, much, much, heavier!"

The younger children gulped. "Th-then what happens?" Freddie stammered.

"Then," the engraver went on, letting his voice rise dramatically, "the die is put in a furnace! The heat makes it soft again."

Bert said, "I'll bet the hub is squeezed into the die again."

"Exactly," Mr. Wilson replied. "You catch on

fast. Sometimes there are as many as six or seven squeezings to make sure every detail has been impressed into the die. Finally the die is shaped to the exact size needed for a coin or medal. Then it's given a bath in salt, rinsed, and polished. And finally," he said, pausing, "the coin or medal is struck."

Flossie had understood everything up to the very last word. "Why would you hit it?" she asked.

The other engravers laughed loudly, as Mr. Wilson said, "I meant that then and only then could a coin or medal be *made*."

On the way to the next room Freddie whispered to Flossie, "I'm glad I'm Freddie Bobbsey and not a die. I wouldn't want to take a bath in salt!"

Stepping through a door with a sign that read "Clean Room," Freddie squirmed. In front of the children two young women were busy sorting white uniforms. "So you're the famous Bobbsey twins!" one of them said. "We got word you were coming."

She handed each one a uniform and matching cap. "Put these on after you take your shower."

"Not me," Freddie said, holding back. "I don't want to get that salt all over me!"

The woman marched him toward a narrow open closet that separated the outer room from the work area. "Do you want to see what they're doing?" she asked him and pointed to the white-coated figures ahead.

Freddie stepped into the closet. To his surprise, a fine spray of air greeted him from several nozzles. "It tickles!" he said.

"That air shower will remove all lint, dust and hairs from your clothing. We wouldn't want anything like that to get onto the coins and medals."

Nan, Flossie, and Bert followed their brother, then slipped into the white uniforms. With the young woman beside them they walked up and down the aisles of tables. On some were scales where silver blanks were being weighed. On others were small presses where blanks were being placed in plastic holders and designs were being imprinted.

Nan suddenly caught sight of something that confused her. A man speaking to another was at the same time taping a metal disk under a table. "Why would he do that?" she wondered.

At her first chance she sidled up to the table. When she was certain that nobody was paying attention, she carefully removed the disk and peeked at it quickly. The design, a rainbow and a flock of tiny birds flying over it, was scooped out of the hard steel. A medal die!

She was eager to show her find to Bert and the younger detectives but knew she could not risk it.

"How can I put the disk back without being seen?" Nan asked herself. A heavy hand clamped down on her wrist.

"Taking a souvenir home for yourself?" a stern voice asked harshly.

CHAPTER X

TV DETECTIVES

THE man's sharp words cut into Nan. She turned to face her accuser and gasped to herself. Sticking out of the white cap that framed his bony face was a fine wisp of curly red hair!

"He's the man I saw in the window of the cutting room!" she thought.

Freddie and Flossie, who heard the accusation, drew near their sister. "What did you say, sir?" the little boy asked.

In reply the man uncurled Nan's fingers, which were clenched around the metal disk. "Oh!" chorused the young twins.

Bert, who had been watching one of the inspectors examine a medal ready for shipment, joined the group. "What's going on?" he asked, as the room started to buzz with the same question. Then his eyes fell on the precious die.

"I think your sister was planning to take this home," the scrawny man said again.

Without listening to another word, Bert replied, "That's not true. Nan never took anything from anybody in her whole life. I'm sure she can explain."

Somewhat shakily, the girl apologized for having caused any trouble. "I——" She did not know what else to say. Should she reveal what she had seen a few minutes earlier? Should she produce the piece of tape that remained stuck under the table from which she had removed the disk?

Nan was not sure who had put the piece there in secret, because the person's back had been turned toward her. In his concealing uniform, one man could easily be mistaken for another. In any event, she knew he must still be in the room. If the girl detective told everything now, he would mark her and the other twins as his enemies! Then harm might come to them!

Bert urged her to continue. "Go ahead, Nan."

"I wanted to get a closer look at this die, that's all," she said at last.

The reason seemed lame to her but she would not risk putting herself and the other twins in danger. "Or maybe I already have!" she suddenly thought, as the bony-faced man snatched the disk from her hand and walked off. Was he the one who planned to steal the die?

The workers who had been listening returned to their stations. An official-looking man had walked in. "I'll take care of this," he said sternly.

"Can you show us where the special plates are made?" Flossie piped up.

Bending toward her, he gritted his teeth. "Do you know what I will do?"

Flossie edged away. "What?"

"I'm going to personally see you children out the door," he boomed, "and off the premises! I'm the supervisor. Follow me!"

The Bobbseys marched silently past the scales, the tables, and the workers. Quickly their lint-free uniforms were taken off and they were ushered into the corridor. The children did not have a chance to defend themselves.

"Slow down!" a familiar voice called out to them. "Where are you taking these kids?" The question was obviously directed to the supervisor, who was in the lead, his nose high in the air.

Wheeling around on his heels, he stamped loudly. The guard who had befriended the twins when they arrived smiled. "I would like to know where you are going in such a hurry."

When the explanations were given, the supervisor threw up his hands. "They're yours!" he told the guard. "You take care of them!"

"That will be my pleasure," the kind man replied. "Come on, let me show you the best part of this place. Call me Harry."

The twins had had a few close calls during their tour of the company and were thankful to be with somebody they could trust.

"You're a pretty important person around here, aren't you?" Flossie asked, smiling at him.

"Oh, not so important," he replied with a grin. "I just like to make sure everybody is safe in this building." He scratched his head, chuckling. " 'Course, I don't know if I've done such a great job watching out for you."

The twins assured Harry they were used to trouble and that he had come just in time to save them from being chased out of the building.

"We almost got ejected!" Freddie announced.

"You mean evicted," Nan told him.

"Uh-uh," said the little boy, "ejected." Nan sighed.

Halfway down the hall they saw a door marked "Security Control Room." Bert asked what it was.

"This is where I spend most of my day," Harry replied, letting the children in.

Against one wall was a bank of small television screens. On them were views of different areas in the plant. Nan counted the screens aloud. There were thirty-six.

"Wow!" exclaimed Freddie.

A guard seated in front of the broad panel was pushing buttons. As he did so, the pictures changed. "We can watch just about every spot inside the grounds," Harry said. "Would you like to see yourselves on television?"

He pushed a button that had "Rewind" written on it, then another that said "Playback." There, on videotape, were the cutting room and the twins—and then the near accident with the carts.

"Please hold that picture!" Bert exclaimed.

Though it was fuzzy in spots, the boy detective could see a figure against the back wall. The man who had pushed the carts! His shadowy frame was skinny and there seemed to be a slight curl to his hair.

Nan gazed deeply into the picture. "He looks like the man I saw through the window!" she declared. "But how did he get upstairs so fast?"

"What man?" Bert asked.

Neither Freddie nor Flossie knew what their sister was talking about. Nan explained.

"Have you any idea who that man could be?" Bert inquired.

Harry shook his head. "There are so many employees here, several hundred. I doubt that even the people who actually hired him could tell you instantly who he is."

The twins were disappointed, but cheered up

"Please hold that picture!" Bert exclaimed.

when Harry added, "When you do figure it out, we'll have this tape as proof."

Freddie and Flossie loved to watch the man switching the pictures from one place to another. Freddie pretended he was playing on the buttons, lifting one finger up, pushing another one down.

"Would you like to really work the buttons?" the man asked him.

The little boy grinned. The first button he pushed flicked on the camera in the visitors' parking lot.

"That's where we came in," Flossie announced.

"And that's Papa Lasky's car!" her young brother added.

Bert peered at the screen. "I wonder how long he's been waiting for us. We'd better get going." Then he noticed something else on the screen. "Freddie, isn't that the van that tried to run us down last night?"

The boys could not get a full view of it because vehicles parked on either side had blocked it. "He's starting, Bert," Freddie observed.

Smoke puffed from the truck's exhaust pipe. "Maybe we can catch him!" Bert said.

With quick thank-you's to the guard, the children ran out of the building. As they reached the lot, the bells of the carillon started to play a tune. Bert checked his watch. It was noontime. The music was playing on schedule.

Then, seeing the faint trail of smoke left by the vanishing truck, Bert exclaimed, "Oh, nuts!" He had not even been able to check the license plate against the one he remembered.

Freddie continued to watch the van as it turned onto the main road, almost a quarter of a mile from the entrance to the plant. He shook his head, thinking about the twins' luckless day.

He took his time going to Papa Lasky's car, where the others had already piled in.

"What's the matter, Freddie?" his twin asked. "Do you wish you had taken a salt bath?"

The little boy pursed his lips, saying, "Maybe."

Flossie knew he was trying to be funny.

"What's this about a salt bath?" Papa Lasky wanted to know.

Eagerly the twins took turns telling about their adventures. They gave every single detail.

"My, my, my," Papa Lasky said, holding his plump face with both hands. "I should never have let you go. I thought I was in trouble, but you——"

His gestures made the children laugh. "Good detectives always find trouble. That's their job," Nan put in.

Papa Lasky said, "My dear, have you ever heard the phrase, 'Never trouble trouble till trouble troubles you?'"

None of the twins had. Bert said they had a

different slogan. "Always trouble trouble till trouble goes away!"

Papa Lasky was shaking his head from side to side as he turned on the ignition. "I'm going to take you all home to lunch," he declared.

Nan agreed that this was a good idea. "We do much better detective work when our tummies are full," she said.

Papa Lasky raised his eyebrows. "More work? Haven't you done enough?"

The children giggled.

"By the way," he continued, "while you were solving my mystery, I bought a plane ticket for Tanya."

Flossie, yawning, said, "Where is she going?"

"Home."

That snapped everybody awake. "Home?" the twins cried. "When?"

"In a few days!"

CHAPTER XI

SURPRISES!

"OH NO!" the Bobbseys exclaimed when they heard that Tanya would be leaving shortly.

"Papa Lasky, please don't send her home," Flossie begged. "She's our friend."

Freddie chimed in, "Please don't."

Papa Lasky backed the car out of the parking space before replying. He glanced in the rear-view mirror at Nan, who was murmuring something to Flossie. The little girl was wiping her eyes with a tissue.

Papa Lasky knew the children would be unhappy about his decision. "There's nothing else I can do," he said. "Please try to understand."

Gloom filled the car as its driver pulled onto the main road. The snow on the highway had fully melted under the strong rays of the sun. On each side, however, snow was banked high against the curb. It seemed to be inviting the children to come out and play in it. But just then the twins were not interested.

Papa Lasky thought he ought to break the silence. He said, "This morning someone phoned our house and warned us to leave town. Tanya took the call."

Bert immediately asked if Mr. Lasky had been there. "No, I didn't go home after I dropped you off. I went downtown and called my wife from there. She told me about it," the man answered. "You see now why I can't let Tanya stay here. It's not safe for any of us."

The twins wondered who had made the phone call to the Laskys.

A possibility occurred to Nan. "Do you suppose it's somebody who works at Silver Town Mint? Maybe he blames you for everything that has happened there. But how could he?"

She did not really expect anyone to answer the baffling question, except perhaps Bert. Her twin suggested that the person might have been an employee who had lost his job and taken his anger out on the Laskys.

"If the company is starting to feel the results of

customers' complaints," he continued, "maybe it will begin laying off more employees."

Papa Lasky did not enter the discussion again. He followed the road to a traffic light and turned onto a side street that led away from the Silver Town section of Lakeport. Bert told him where the Bobbsey house was located.

Within a half hour they turned into the driveway, which had been neatly cleared. Tire marks in the snow told the children their father had probably driven the small van to his lumberyard.

"Daddy works very hard," said Flossie. She told Papa Lasky what Mr. Bobbsey did.

The man seemed impressed. "Your father is lucky to have his own business. I wish I did too. I would never have gotten into this mess," he said, letting the car's engine idle while the twins got out.

When she saw the unfamiliar vehicle pull up to the house, Mrs. Bobbsey went to the door. Bert was holding the front seat forward so that Nan and Flossie could step out onto the snowy pavement.

"Nan! Bert! Freddie! Flossie!" the attractive woman called out. "Ask Mr. Lasky to come inside."

With some urging, he shut off the ignition and followed the twins into the house. Nan introduced him.

Mrs. Bobbsey shook his hand and thanked him. Then she examined the children's coats, Bert's and Freddie's especially, before hanging them up.

"These look as if they had been through a few cycles in the washing machine!"

Freddie glanced up at his mother. "We did take air showers!"

Mrs. Bobbsey patted her son's curls, which had flattened under the wool cap she now put on a shelf in the closet. "In your coat, dear?"

He nodded.

It was time for a talk about the children's adventures since they had left for the Freedom Day program at Silver Town School. Even Mr. Lasky, who had settled into the comfortable leather lounging chair in a corner of the living room, was amazed to hear each twin's version.

"You certainly should be very proud of them," Papa Lasky said to Mrs. Bobbsey. Her face beamed when he described Bert and Freddie's brave rescue.

The younger twins now gave the news that worried them most. Mrs. Bobbsey was sorry to learn that Tanya might have to leave the States.

"Not might, but will!" Papa Lasky said firmly.

Sensing that this was the last thing the Laskys wanted, Mrs. Bobbsey offered an idea. "Why not let Tanya stay with us until your problems are straightened out?"

Flossie hugged her mother. "That's creamy, Mommy!" she bubbled.

Papa Lasky was evidently touched by the suggestion but said, "No, that would be too much to ask of you."

Appealing to reason, the twins' mother went on, "It would only be fair. After all, you and your wife kindly took care of our four children and on one of the worst nights of the year. We would love to have Tanya spend some time with us."

The sad expression on Mr. Lasky's face changed to a glow of happiness. "Now I know the secret of where the twins get their convincing ways," he said. "Mrs. Bobbsey, I am so grateful."

Flossie hopped off her mother's knee and bounced toward the man. "You're going to let Tanya stay with us? You are? You are? It's so 'citing!"

Papa Lasky tweaked the little girl's nose, then asked if he might use the phone to contact his wife. Shortly he reached her. "Dear, I have some fantastic news," he said but was cut off by Mrs. Lasky. "What?" he asked. "Where did she go?" His voice, which had been calm, now became panicky. He hung up the phone, quivering.

The others, having heard the rising volume of his voice, jumped up. "What's the matter?" Freddie asked.

Papa Lasky's face had drained white. "Tanya has run away!" he said in a daze. "She's gone!"

Bert led the man to the leather chair. "Tell us everything," he urged.

Mr. Lasky explained. "My wife told Tanya about the plane ticket. We don't have much money. I drew a lot from the savings account to pay for the one-way fare." He put his head in his hands. "I don't understand. I don't understand," he said over and over. Looking up once again, he added, "She took the silver-bell plate with her, too."

That gave Bert a hunch. "Would you drive us to the Lakeport Museum?" he asked the girl's American father.

Still somewhat bewildered, Papa Lasky did not hear the question. Bert repeated it. This time the man's face filled with a rosy color.

"You want to go to a silly museum when our Tanya is missing!" he burst out in anger. He would not let the boy explain, abruptly requesting his coat and saying a curt good-by to Mrs. Bobbsey.

As he stormed out of the house, the twins' mouths fell open in disbelief. Freddie and Flossie dashed to the door, calling to him to come back. But the car engine started, its wheels spinning on the hardened snow. Papa Lasky shot out of the driveway.

"*Tanya has run away!*" *Papa Lasky said.*

Mrs. Bobbsey closed the front door, saying, "I can drive you downtown."

Bert did not tell anyone what his hunch was, and he decided to hold off until the children reached the museum.

"Aren't you going to tell us why we're going there?" Nan asked her twin. "Are we supposed to guess?"

Bert winked.

"Do you want to show us some old dime-store bones?" Flossie piped up.

"You mean dinosaur bones?" Bert asked.

The little girl smiled. "That's what I said—dime-store bones."

"No," was Bert's reply, but he said no more.

"Miss Widget told us," Freddie put in, "that there are some nice pictures hanging there. Want to see those?"

"Uh-huh, but not today," his brother answered.

Nan had not offered a guess. "It must have something to do with Tanya or the plate!" she declared. "But I can't imagine what you hope to discover." She eyed Bert, thinking he might break down and tell them.

But the boy did not relent. When they were ready to leave, he helped the girls into their coats and handed Freddie's boots to him. Nan opened the door. A waft of cold air blew inside.

"Brr-brr!" Flossie cried out. She was behind

Nan. "Ooh, let's hurry to the car and put the heat on," she said.

Nan did not budge at first. She bent down outside the door and picked up a medium-sized carton that lay on the welcome mat.

"What's that?" the others asked.

"It's addressed to the Bobbsey kids," Nan replied and showed everybody the package.

"Open it! Open it!" Flossie said eagerly.

Their mother glanced at her watch. "You won't have much time to spend at the museum if we don't leave right now."

Without another word the twins went to the station wagon. Nan clutched the lightweight carton. Strong cord had been tied around it several times and thick tape was attached at each end and down the middle.

"I don't know if I can open this," Nan said. "Here, Bert, maybe you can with your penknife."

As Mrs. Bobbsey started the car, Bert fished in his pocket for the knife. "I wonder who sent this to us," he said.

In the corner of the package was a brief return address containing a post-office box number but no name.

"Maybe there's a card inside," Nan suggested.

Her twin twisted his face into a frown as he cut down through the tape that sealed the package. It was tough and thick. Finally he opened the lid.

Bert turned to Nan. "It's only fair that you be the first to see what's inside."

Nan lifted the close-fitting top of an inner box. "Wow!" she exclaimed.

There were twelve silver bells with leather handles, each one a different size. They sparkled in the sunlight as Freddie and Flossie picked up two and rang them gently.

"They are bee-yoo-ti-ful!" exclaimed the little girl as the one in her hand tinkled in a high, clear tone.

Nan discovered a piece of paper folded in the empty space and opened it. A message! She read it to herself and gasped.

"Come on, Nan! What does it say?" Freddie demanded.

CHAPTER XII

LIBERTY BELL LULU

WITHOUT reading the message aloud, Nan snatched the bells away from Freddie and Flossie and put them in the box. "This package will have to be mailed back!" she declared.

Bert stretched out his hand for the piece of paper on his sister's lap. He read quickly, "We hope you have fun playing these bells. Don't make trouble for us at the mint. We will send you another surprise soon."

The twins' mother was shocked. "Somebody is trying to bribe you with gifts!" Mrs. Bobbsey exclaimed.

She usually kept cool, even when the young

detectives knew she was angry. This gift had out-
raged her as much as it had her daughter, and
she said so.

Flossie did not quite understand. "They are
trying to make a bride of me?" she asked.

"No, silly," said Nan. "This is somebody's
way of paying us to stop working on the mystery!"

Now that the little girl knew what bribery
meant, she sniffed at the gleaming bells. "Is there
a name on the paper, Bert?" she asked.

Mrs. Bobbsey had been wondering the same
thing. Bert said there was nothing written after
the message or in it to indicate who had sent the
carton.

"It doesn't matter," Nan said with a touch of
emotion in her voice. "We can repack it and
send it to the box number."

Bert, on the other hand, said he would like
to study the bells more closely before returning
them. "We might find a clue to the person who
sent them." The others agreed.

When they reached the museum, a circular
building with a cone-shaped roof, Nan slid the
box under the front seat. Mrs. Bobbsey said she
had some shopping to attend to and would meet
the children in half an hour.

The twins thanked her for the lift and piled
out of the car. Small peaks of snow lined the solid
stone railing that curved up to the main entrance.

A white banner with dark-blue letters on it flapped against the top of the doorway.

"AMERICA, WE SALUTE YOU!" Bert read the banner, as the others looked up at it. "Every museum in the nation is having special exhibits about the U.S.A."

The country's birthday celebration had officially started on the first day of January. Lakeport like all American cities and towns, had planned various events to honor the year, including parades and patriotic concerts.

The Lakeport Museum had grown tremendously, just as the city had. The original building had not been large enough to house the many paintings and art objects brought to it from around the world. The new structure, recently completed, was a beautiful landmark in the city.

As the twins entered, they stopped to admire the effect of sunlight filtered through a colored window in the high ceiling. Wide corridors branched off in several directions, radiating like numbers on a clock.

"Where are we going?" Flossie whispered to Bert.

He had noticed a sign pointing toward an outer room. In large bold letters it said SPECIAL EXHIBITS. He motioned everyone to follow. Nan took the young twins' hands.

Gold rope had been strung between several

short metal poles in the room they entered. "What's that for?" Freddie asked.

"To keep the crowds in line," Nan offered.

Freddie replied that he did not see many people.

"That's because of the snow. A lot of folks wouldn't bother to come here today," Nan explained.

As Bert led them into the room, they passed tall, sparkling glass cases that displayed uniforms of American soldiers. They ranged from present-day military dress to that worn years ago.

Flossie pulled on Nan to make her stop walking. She gazed at a light-tan dress and a small hat tilted downward to the right with an insignia on it.

"That's a WAC," she said, reading the card on the floor of the case. "She's a wicwac!"

The "she" Flossie referred to was a wire figure whose meshlike hand was raised in an army salute. Flossie stood straight and put her chubby fingers to her forehead. "I'm Flossie Wac." She giggled.

Realizing that Bert had gone on ahead of them, Nan grabbed Flossie's hand and hurried the young twins along. "I don't know what Bert has in mind," she said, "but I don't want to miss it!"

Neither did Freddie and Flossie. Their brother finally stopped. He was standing in front of a

"I'm Flossie Wac." The little girl giggled.

glass case that extended to the low ceiling. As the others caught up to him, they spied a broad grin on his face. In a second they knew why.

Displayed on black velvet were replicas of famous bells known throughout the world, chief among them, the Liberty Bell. Beneath them was something more fantastic—a silver plate with the Liberty Bell engraved on the front. It was identical to Tanya's!

"Wowee!" exclaimed Freddie. He was, like the others, entranced by the beauty of the display.

On the card next to the plate was written, "This is a copy of a plate cast on March 4, 1846, to commemorate the Liberty Bell, which rang its last clear note that year."

Flossie wanted to know if this was the Laskys' plate. "What do you think, Bert?" she asked.

Her brother ruffled her hair, which curled around the edge of her winter hat. "That's just what I think," he said mysteriously, adding, "I have a hunch Tanya brought the plate here."

"Then you don't think she ran away?" Nan asked.

Bert said he doubted that possibility. "Where would she go?" he asked. "She was sure the plate belonged to the museum even if it was not the original!"

"Wow! You're a quick thinker!" Freddie exclaimed.

One thing troubled Nan. Why had the plate been so quickly placed into the display case? If Tanya had brought it to the museum that morning, would the curator have had time to mark the plate, classify it, and have someone type the card? She knew all these steps were necessary before an item could be shown to the public.

Nan did not voice her doubt aloud, however. "Where to now, Bert?" she asked.

He snapped his fingers. "Let's find the curator," he said.

Freddie was not eager to hurry off. He had barely enough time to look at the beautiful things in the case. "Nan, stay with me a little while," he said, "and tell me what all the cards say."

They decided that Flossie would accompany Bert to the curator's office while the other two would spend a few more minutes studying the exhibit.

"We'll meet you in the center hall. Okay?" Bert suggested, turning on his heel.

For a moment Nan stood quietly reading the long paragraph printed on the clear plastic sign. It hung on the inner wall of the case and gave the history of bells.

"Primitive man probably discovered the bell by accident. Perhaps he was working with metals and struck a metal dish, causing the first bell tone," Nan repeated aloud. "True bell-making, however, did not begin until man learned to make bronze by mixing copper and tin."

While Nan was speaking, Freddie's eyes focused on a square-shaped bell in the case. It was about six inches high and almost five inches wide. It consisted of two bent plates fastened together with iron rivets and was coated in bronze.

"That is one of the oldest bells ever found," Nan said, reading the card next to it. "Supposedly St. Patrick used it to scare all the snakes out of Ireland!"

Freddie laughed. "It must have made a terrible racket!" he exclaimed.

The bell placed next to it was a replica of another one, now hanging in a pagoda in Burma in the Pacific Ocean. Nan said, "The real one is a hundred thousand times bigger. It weighs ninety tons and can hold fifty people inside!"

"Wow!" her brother declared, then glanced at another replica on display. "Tell me about this one, Nan."

The girl said it was a Russian bell and nicknamed Big John because it was so huge. It weighs 260,000 pounds. "In 1737 it was hung in a wooden tower at one end of the Kremlin. A fire broke out in the belfry and before anyone could stop the fire, the timbers that supported the bell burned. Big John fell hard and dug thirty feet into the ground!"

Freddie listened in awe. "Is that how the Liberty Bell cracked?" he asked.

Nan said no. "That happened when it was first hung in the State House in Philadelphia. Some unnamed person grasped the heavy clapper, pulled it toward him and let it fly to the opposite edge of the brim. There was a loud bong followed by a low hum and then a crack that split the brim. Nobody knows exactly why that happened. Maybe the metal was too brittle or maybe during a storm at sea when a ship was carrying it from England to Philadelphia, the bell suffered a major blow that left the metal weak."

Freddie asked if the bell could be rung after it cracked.

"Yes, but first it had to be melted down and recast," Nan said, then added, "The Liberty Bell had another bad shock when it fell from a wagon."

Her brother wanted to hear all the details and was surprised to learn that when the British marched into Philadelphia they had hoped to steal all the bells in the city, including the Liberty Bell.

"That's a lulu of a story!" the little boy declared.

"The soldiers wanted to use the bell metal for musket shot," Nan explained, "but an American, Colonel Flower, ordered that all the bells be removed from the city. The Liberty Bell was to be taken to Bethlehem, Pennsylvania, on an Army wagon. The wagon probably collapsed under the weight of the heavy object."

Freddie asked her, "Did it break then, too?"

"Yes, but not right away. The shock of the fall no doubt had weakened the bell and when it was rung years later, it split open in a wide crack."

In the meantime Bert and Flossie had been directed to an office on the second floor. They could hear typing on the other side of the door marked OFFICE OF THE CURATOR. Entering, they smiled at the young man seated behind a large oval desk piled high with papers.

"Are you the curator?" Bert asked.

A smile greeted the question. "No, I'm his assistant. May I help you?" He pushed back the large horn-rimmed glasses that covered half his face, and rubbed his eyes.

"It's important that we speak with the curator," Bert said. "We don't have much time."

The pleasant man quipped, "Trying to catch a train or something?"

"No," Bert replied politely, "a ride home."

"I see," the fellow said. "Well, if you tell me what's so important, possibly I can take care of the matter."

Bert insisted that he wanted to talk to the curator. The assistant sighed and dialed the phone beside him. "Someone is with him now," he told the boy, "but I'll ask him."

He conveyed Bert's message, then holding his hand over the receiver, asked, "What do you wish to see him about?"

All Bert replied was, "A silver plate."

Shortly the young detectives were ushered into the adjoining room. Both could have leaped happily when they stepped in. There, talking with the curator, was the missing Tanya! Her back was turned to the Bobbseys, but they could not mistake the figure and the long brown hair.

"How do you do?" the distinguished-looking man said to Bert and Flossie.

Tanya turned around. She was surprised to see them too but no more than they were to see what she was holding. It was the silver-bell plate!

CHAPTER XIII

MUSEUM MISHAP

"TANYA!" Bert and Flossie cried out when they saw her in the curator's office. Flossie hugged her.

Bert quickly explained to the curator, who had stood up to greet his visitors, that they had been searching for Tanya. "I knew you didn't run away," Bert said to the girl.

"Run away?" Tanya repeated.

Flossie told her that Mama Lasky was worried. "She'll be so happy to see you."

The curator interrupted briefly. "Please sit down, all of you," he said kindly.

Flossie squeezed herself next to Tanya in the large swivel chair, while Bert took the matching one. Tanya held the plate close to her, glancing at it now and then, as she gave her reasons for being at the museum.

"I came to find out how much this plate is worth. I thought maybe the museum would like to buy it in place of the one that was stolen."

The curator had a thick manilla folder in front of him. He read a piece of paper that had some kind of list on it.

Bert glanced at the nameplate on the man's desk. "Mr. Dobie," he said, "would the museum like to have an extra copy of this bell plate?"

"An *extra* copy?" Tanya asked Bert.

Flossie piped up, "There's a plate just like yours in the big room downstairs!"

It seemed to all who watched her that Tanya was ready to break into tears. Instead, she smiled at Mr. Dobie. "I am sorry I have troubled you," she said, and rose.

To Bert and Flossie she added, "I overheard Mama Lasky talking to Papa on the telephone this morning about my trip home, and how much it would cost. I thought maybe I could surprise them and pay for it."

The curator pushed his papers aside, saying, "Oh, my dear, that plate could buy you at most only three or four cokes. It looks like silver but it is nothing more than a platinum overglaze on ceramic."

Tanya sank back into her chair, edging Flossie out of it.

Flossie was angry. "We want to find the first-first plate!" she exclaimed.

"Oh, you do," Mr. Dobie said with a grin. "How do you think you will locate the original, if the police can't do it?"

Ignoring the remark, Bert asked him, "I would like to know about the Liberty Bell plate you have on display now. It seems to be an exact copy of this one."

Mr. Dobie settled back in his broad tweedy chair. "A short time ago I requested the Silver Town Mint Center to make a pure silver plate identical to the one stolen. Instead of that, we received a fake, an excellent one, mind you. But it was a fake. I suppose you've heard the recent charges against the company."

The twins nodded but did not offer any comment. They were very interested in what the curator had told them.

"Is the plate in the exhibit made of the same material as this one?" Bert asked.

He motioned to Tanya to hand the man the one in her hands. Weighing it on one palm, Mr. Dobie declared, "I would say yes. I imagine that this was also produced by the mint. Another phony."

Bert quickly pointed out that there was no definite proof the firm had produced phony items.

"Then how would you explain my order?" the

curator said, referring to the plate again. "It was sent directly here from the Silver Town Mint address. I'm sure nobody made an exchange on the way."

Flossie and Bert felt that it was useless to try convincing the man that fake items were not being ordered by the management. The children would have to reveal what they suspected: that someone was trying to make an innocent company look guilty.

As Bert and Tanya rose to say good-by, Flossie noticed that the door behind them was slightly open. Part of a face showed. Someone was listening on the other side! Who was it?

The little girl darted to the door and pulled it wide, "Oh!" she screeched, seeing a red-haired man in dark-green work clothes crouched outside.

Tanya and Bert pivoted. Instantly the boy recognized the figure he had seen on the security TV screen. He was the one who had tried to mow down the twins with carts of silver!

The man seemed stunned for a split second. Then he dashed through the outer office past the assistant's unoccupied desk.

"Wait a minute! Stop!" Bert shouted, racing after him.

Mr. Dobie, who was not more than a head taller than Tanya, tried to see over hers as she

"Stop!" Bert shouted.

followed Bert and Flossie. "What's going on here?" he demanded.

The children had dashed out of his room before he knew why. The red-haired man hurried along the marble railing that circled the second floor, and into a narrow corridor lined with statues. Once he looked back to see if the children were still on his trail. They were! He turned a corner and ducked into an alcove.

As the children reached the spot, they lost sight of him. They halted to catch their breath, then started to retrace their steps. In a flash the man left the curved niche and dashed off again.

"There he is!" Bert cried.

Though Tanya had not shared any of the twins' adventures at the Silver Town Mint, she ran as hard as the others after the man. He led them through another narrow hallway with stone figures on pedestals down the center.

Behind them voices shouted, "Stop those children!"

Flossie cocked her head to one side. A museum guard was running after her, his arms stretched out for the catch. "Ooh-eee!" she exclaimed and skidded into one of the pedestals.

The small figure on top wobbled. Before anyone could stop it, the statue crashed to the floor! Flossie, who had bounced back onto a small velvet-cushioned bench, gasped.

The guard glared at her. "Your daddy will pay for this!"

He started to sweep the tiny fragments out of the aisle. Bert and Tanya, hearing the loud noise, gave up their chase and darted back to Flossie. She was crying. "I slipped," she said. "I didn't mean to do it."

Bert put an arm around her. "Don't worry," he said.

"Wh-where did Red go?" she asked.

Tanya sat down next to the little girl. "I'm sure he is out of the building by now."

Flossie wiped her eyes. "It's all my fault," she said. "We could have caught him, Bert!"

Mr. Dobie walked swiftly toward the children. "I'll take care of this," he said to the guard. He bent down to Flossie. "Are you all right, honey?"

The little girl nodded, sniffling.

Bert asked, "How can we pay you for the broken statue, Mr. Dobie?"

Just then Nan and Freddie appeared at the end of the hallway. They had waited a long time for Bert and Flossie in the center lobby, then decided to go to the curator's office. Somebody had told them two children had been seen running up and down the second-floor corridor.

When Nan saw the pieces of the broken statue and the man bending down toward her sister, she hurried to Flossie's side.

Bert said, "We saw the guy who went after us with the carts!"

At once Freddie flexed a muscle in his arm. "Did he hurt my sister?" he asked. "If he did, I'll —— I'll——"

Mr. Dobie stood up. "Please tell me whom you are talking about and why you have disrupted my museum."

First Bert apologized for what had occurred, then he described the episode at the Silver Town Mint earlier that morning.

"Do you know who that red-haired man is?" he asked.

Mr. Dobie shrugged. "I barely saw him. My assistant apparently had to leave for a while, and the stranger entered. I doubt that anybody got a very good look at him."

The Bobbseys wondered why the red-haired man was not at work. And how did he know the twins were at the museum?

Nan suggested one answer. "Maybe he isn't the person you think he is," she said mysteriously.

Freddie scratched his head. "Huh?" he asked. "But Bert and Flossie saw him."

"I know," Nan said, "but I think there are two men who look very much alike. In fact, they might be twins!"

The idea astounded the others, but there was no time to discuss it further. Bert had checked his watch. No doubt Mrs. Bobbsey was waiting for them in the car.

Before leaving, the children requested Mr. Dobie to send a bill to their home for the broken statue. The curator said it would be impossible to determine the value.

"Besides, I think Patrick Henry," he said, referring to the name penned on the base of the bust, "was a gift from our state." In a moment he added, "Do you children know about the famous speech he made in Philadelphia?"

Bert remembered the most famous line. "Give me liberty or give me death!" he said.

Mr. Dobie smiled. "Very good. Well, I think this is the end of *our* Patrick Henry, but don't fret. We'll find another statue to replace it. I'm just glad that none of you were hurt during your great chase."

More than ever, the children wanted to find the original plate of the Liberty Bell to make up for the accident at the museum.

When they stepped outside, a horn honked at them. Mrs. Bobbsey had parked the station wagon several meters away. Seeing a fifth person with the twins, she smiled.

"You must be Tanya Mirov," she said before Nan had a chance to introduce her. "I'm so glad to meet you."

Tanya immediately liked the twins' soft-spoken

mother, who went on, "We would love to have you stay with us a while." She explained that the Laskys were in favor of the idea. "Will you come?"

The girl was thrilled. "Oh yes, yes!" she exclaimed. "Thank you. Thank you."

"In that case," Mrs. Bobbsey said, "I'll drive to your home so you can pick up some clothes."

Although the twins wanted to ask their friend about the threatening phone call and show her the set of bells, they decided to wait. For the first time Tanya seemed genuinely happy. The twins did not want to spoil it.

Mrs. Bobbsey guided her car slowly through the deep puddles and slushy streets. Finally they reached the Silver Town section of Lakeport. When they pulled up to the Lasky home, the couple's car was not there.

One after the other, the children piled out of the station wagon and went to the front door. Tanya rang the bell. There was no answer.

Bert announced that a basement window was open. Mrs. Bobbsey, who had stayed in the car, watched her son start to climb through it. She rolled down her window to ask why he was doing this.

"The front door is locked," Bert reported.

In a few moments he opened the door. Mrs. Bobbsey and the children entered the house. Nan went upstairs with Tanya to help her pack. As the Lasky's young daughter pulled her small suitcase from under the bed, a noise clattered overhead.

"Maybe Mama's cleaning up there," the girl said. "We did make a mess."

Gaily she climbed the narrow stairway to the attic. "Is that you Mama? It's Tanya!" She pushed the door open, then cried out, "Oh, no!"

CHAPTER XIV

THE SILVER CLUE

TANYA's cry carried down the stairwell. Nan, who was just lifting her friend's suitcase onto a small rack, dropped it. She ran up the steps and called out to Bert to come too.

"Oh!" Nan exclaimed when she reached the landing.

The attic workroom was a wreck. A box of tools on the metal table had been dumped. They had rolled and fallen to the floor. Most of the small cartons in the corners had been torn apart. They held bundles of personal papers.

"Who could do such a thing?" Tanya asked in dismay. She was about to pick up some of the tools when Nan stopped her.

"The police will want to look for fingerprints," she said.

Bert had heard Nan's call and ran up quickly. "What's the matter?" he asked.

When he saw the room, Bert went at once to the first floor to telephone the police. Outside, a car was pulling into the driveway. The chugging engine stopped and doors opened.

"It's Mama and Papa!" Tanya exclaimed, looking out a window. She hurried down the stairs.

Bert in the meantime had dialed the police. But when the Laskys came in, they did not pay much attention to the boy using the phone. They were too happy to see Tanya.

"Why did you run away?" Mama Lasky asked her. Then, kissing the girl's forehead, she added, "You must never do that again!"

Tanya tried to explain what she had done but could not get a word in, as the couple chatted happily. Finally Tanya caught sight of Bert, who had put down the phone.

Papa Lasky patted the boy on the back. "You children are absolutely amazing!" he said. "Somehow I really believe you are going to solve my mystery!"

Bert knew that the man's mood would change swiftly when he went to the attic. "Mr. Lasky," the boy detective said slowly.

"What is it, son?" Tanya's father asked. "Speak up."

Bert took a deep breath. "We have something to show you."

The couple followed Bert upstairs. When they saw what had happened, the Laskys gasped. Bert had expected Papa to burst into a rage but he did not do so. He stood quietly gazing at the wreck. His wife slipped her arm through his.

"The police are on their way," Bert said, leading the couple down to the living room again. He now introduced his mother to the Laskys.

Freddie and Flossie had wanted to go to the attic also, but Mrs. Bobbsey had kept them with her. Nan described the mess on the third floor.

"How dreadful!" Mrs. Bobbsey remarked.

Apparently the intruder had a special reason for ransacking the attic. But what was it? The Bobbseys tried to figure out the motive.

Bert said to Papa Lasky, "You told us you did not know who rented this house before you moved in. Correct?"

The man nodded.

"What would someone be looking for in that room?" Bert went on.

Both the Laskys shrugged.

Nan said that it did not seem as if anything had been stolen. She looked at her twin. "Do you suppose it was done to frighten the Laskys?"

Bert did not think so. "Then, why didn't the intruder mess up the rest of the house?"

The only answer Nan could think of was, "Maybe he saw us driving up and took off."

Just then the front doorbell rang. A tall, sturdily built policeman stood there. He introduced himself as Officer Burley and entered. The next few moments were spent in introductions.

The policeman looked at the twins. "At headquarters we hear a lot about you Bobbseys," the officer said with a grin.

"I hope it's all good!" Mrs. Bobbsey put in with a wink.

"It sure is," the officer replied.

He now asked if he might look around the house. "Everything seems to be in order in this room," he said. "I'd like to see the second and third floors."

Bert had described the condition of the attic over the phone. He volunteered to take the policeman up to it. Mr. Lasky followed.

"May I go too?" Freddie asked.

Officer Burley said he would like to have the company of such fine detectives. "You can help me hunt for clues."

"I want to go too," Flossie said, but her mother thought the policeman would have enough help from the other children.

Taking two steps at a time, the policeman reached the second floor quickly. Freddie wanted to be like him. Holding the stairway railing, he poised his foot for a leap to the third step. He missed it, slipping back to the second one. He was not ready to give up trying the broad jumps and made another attempt, but failed again. "Oops!" Freddie exclaimed.

Bert, who was at the top of the stairway, turned around. "Come on, slowpoke!" he called.

Without any more jumps, the little boy scurried up to his brother. The policeman began glancing into the rooms on the second floor. Now and then he would bend down to pick up a piece of thread or a tiny pin.

Very few words were exchanged among the searchers. Freddie stayed close to the officer. He mimicked every movement the man made. At one point the policeman got down on his hands and knees and ran one hand over the carpet. Freddie did the same, though he did not know what Officer Burley was looking for.

"Am I doing it right?" the little boy asked, continuing to feel the rug with his fingers.

Burley chuckled. He explained that he had detected a slight stain in the material and wondered if it might be a recent wet boot print. "It's not, though, just some liquid that was spilled."

At this moment the telephone rang. Mr. Lasky went to the first floor to answer it.

In the meantime Bert had gone to the attic. When Officer Burley and Freddie joined him,

"Oops!" Freddie exclaimed.

Bert was examining a patch of dark-green nylon material.

As the others drew close, he said, "I'll bet this comes from the clothes of the man who was here. It looks like a piece torn from a windbreaker."

"Or maybe a work uniform," Freddie added. "I see something shiny stuck on it."

Officer Burley took the cloth from Bert and with a pair of fine tweezers removed a tiny sliver caught in the material. "It's some sort of metal," he said.

The two boys instantly thought of silver. "Maybe it's a shaving of silver!" Bert said.

He and Freddie had the same idea at once. Somebody from the Silver Town Mint had broken into the Lasky home! But why?

Downstairs, Papa Lasky was talking on the phone. Flossie had run out to meet him and was holding his free hand tightly. But Papa Lasky ignored her. He listened a while to the caller, then answered.

"Tomorrow afternoon? I'll be there." He hung up.

When he and Flossie returned to the living room, Officer Burley was there with Bert and Freddie.

"We'll do all we can for you," the policeman promised Mr. and Mrs. Lasky. He said good-by and left.

Mrs. Bobbsey thought it was time for her and the children to leave also. "Are you ready, Tanya?" she asked.

The girl hurried to her room and within fifteen minutes was at the front door, wearing her coat and boots. Her suitcase was in one hand.

Her American father seemed to have recovered from the shock of what had occurred in the attic. "Have a good time, dear," he said to the girl and hugged her. "You didn't take the plate with you, did you, Tanya?" he asked.

"No, Papa Lasky."

"Good."

The Bobbseys thought this was an odd question. After all, why would Tanya carry the plate with the Freedom Bell on it out of the Lasky house a second time?

On the way to their own home the Bobbseys talked of nothing but the mystery. Bert and Freddie told the others about the clue of the nylon patch and the metallic sliver they were sure was a piece of silver.

Flossie giggled. "Sliver silver, sliver silver, silly silver sliver, sippy siffer sliver. I mean, sipper sliffy siver. I mean, siffy siffer siffer."

Everybody laughed as the little girl tried to say the words faster and faster, getting more mixed up each time.

"You're sliffy! I mean, silly, Flossie!" said Freddie.

"You can't say it real fast either," was his twin's reply.

That nettled Freddie. "So what?" he said. "I can too. Silver silver silver."

Flossie giggled harder. "See? It's sil——" She sneezed.

Mrs. Bobbsey handed her a tissue. "I hope you haven't caught cold."

Flossie sneezed again. As she held the tissue to her nose, she leaned against Freddie and whispered.

"I heard Papa Lasky talking on the phone. I think it was to a man. He had a real deep voice. I heard the man say to Papa, 'Slipper-mint Carlon.'"

CHAPTER XV

DING-DONG DUMMY

NAN and Bert wanted to know what Flossie was whispering to Freddie. "Now who's keeping secrets?" the older boy teased.

Flossie nodded, but immediately sneezed again. Freddie had not understood everything she told him. The tissue she was using had muffled her voice.

"It has something to do with the car being on," the little boy replied.

That did not make sense to his listeners, but they did not ask any more questions. When they reached home, Dinah opened the door. She and her husband, Sam, had lived with the Bobbseys since Bert and Nan were born.

"Well I'm sure glad you honeys are safe," she said. "I say to Sam all the time, 'I hope those blessed young detectives are keeping out of trouble.' "

The twins laughed, then introduced Tanya. Dinah shook hands and said, "My, you're pretty." She grinned. "But you're kind of thin. You need some of Dinah Johnson's good cooking!"

Flossie said, "Dinah's the best cook in America!" The others smiled.

Bert carried Tanya's bag upstairs, and Nan showed their young visitor to the guest room. Tanya admired it, then said, "I am tired. May I take a nap?"

"Of course," Nan replied. "Come downstairs after you wake up."

The four twins gathered in the living room. "Now tell us what you heard on the Laskys' phone," Bert urged Flossie.

The little girl stumbled over the words, Slippermint Carlon.

Nan corrected her. "The man on the phone must've said Silver Mint Carillon."

Bert agreed. "Did you hear anything else?" he asked his sister.

Flossie mumbled no and yawned.

"I hope everybody is free tomorrow afternoon," Bert said. He winked at the other detectives.

The twins decided not to tell Tanya what they planned to do. They did not want to worry her.

"Besides," Nan said, "she has been through a lot since the school bus broke down. I think Tanya ought to take it easy."

When they had a chance, Bert and Nan told their mother and father about the girl's heart condition. Mrs. Bobbsey said she would watch Tanya closely.

"By the way," she added, "have you forgotten about something?"

The foursome did not think so until Mrs. Bobbsey took a carton from the closet. "The bells," she said.

She was amazed that none of the twins leaped for the package. Nan, who had wanted to mail the box back as soon as possible, yawned. Bert said he was exhausted.

"Let's study them tomorrow," he suggested.

Mrs. Bobbsey was puzzled but said nothing.

The next morning the sky was as blue as the ocean on which the twins had sailed in summer. Pockets of water where snow had melted the day before were partly frozen. Under the sun's hot rays the ice would turn into water again.

Bert carried the carton of handbells into the living room, where the other children had gathered. Freddie and Flossie reached for the smaller ones they had played with earlier.

"Ding, ding, ding," the little girl sang. She slipped her chubby hand through the leather handle and swung the silver bell gently.

"Dong, dong, dong," her twin sang. He rang his bell, then picked up two more.

Meanwhile Nan and Bert were examining the other bells closely for clues that might reveal the identity of the sender. Tanya was so impressed by the beautiful sounds, she came downstairs. When she learned the twins' suspicion that the bells had been sent to them as a bribe, she was dismayed.

"You mean somebody is afraid you might learn the truth," she said keenly, "so he bribed you with a beautiful gift."

She could not resist holding two of the delicate bells that gleamed brightly. She swung one, then another in a simple rhythm.

"The song is from my country. It has only two tones," she said.

As Tanya played the short piece again, the young twins joined in. When they finished, Tanya chose another bell, slightly larger than either of those she had rung before.

"This one should have a deeper sound," she said and swung it back.

The clapper, a short metal stick with a tiny ball at the end, hit the shell with a dull thud.

Tanya swung the handle forward, letting the

clapper fall against the other side. The same thing happened.

"Something is wrong with this bell," she said. "It not ring."

Flossie put in, "You discovered a ding-dong dummy!"

Tanya was disappointed until Bert added, "That may be the biggest clue anybody has found yet!"

The foreign girl smiled. "I am so glad!" she said. "What does it tell you?"

Bert thought a moment. "So far nothing, but maybe it will!" he replied mysteriously. He told the others what he had in mind. "Let's take this funny bell to the Pied Piper Music Shop."

Although Tanya said she would like to accompany the others, she thought it best if she stayed at home and rested.

Nan said, "I've changed my mind about returning these bells right away. I suppose we ought to keep them as evidence." Bert agreed.

Mrs. Bobbsey said she had a few errands to do downtown that would not take long. "I'll be glad to drop you four off at the music shop. You can take a bus home."

When the twins later stepped inside the glass-front building, a gentle-faced man in a royal-blue suit greeted them. "May I help you?" he asked.

At first the children did not reply. They were

"You discovered a ding-dong dummy!" Flossie said.

awed by the sparkling array of musical instruments. There were golden trumpets in red velvet-lined cases, black clarinets with shiny silver buttons, several guitars, and a small organ with pearl-white keys.

Flossie pressed one key but there was no sound. "This is another ding-dong dummy," she said.

The man rubbed his hands nervously as the children wandered around. He particularly watched Flossie, who was trying to play the little organ. She hit the keys harder but still no sound came out.

"I'm Mr. Platt," he said, plugging in a wire cord. "And that," he added as Flossie shattered the air with a loud blast on the instrument, "is an electric organ!"

The little twin instantly lifted her fingers off the keys. "It isn't a ding-dong dummy after all?" she asked.

The man, confused, said, "A what?"

Flossie hurried to Bert and took the bag he was carrying. She pulled out the bell that did not ring.

Mr. Platt eyed it with interest. "May I?" he asked and accepted the bell.

"Can you make it work?" Flossie asked.

By now the other children had gathered around the pair. "Can you?" Flossie repeated.

Mr. Platt swung the handle, then tapped the

outer shell. "Sorry," he said. "This bell isn't made of bronze. I think it's pure silver."

Everybody was amazed. "Why would anybody make a bell that can't ring?" Nan asked.

The store owner suggested that the piece might have been created for decoration only. "It certainly is beautiful, even if it doesn't make a sound," he said, handing it back to Flossie.

Bert thought that while they were there, he should find out more about carillons. "Do you know anything about them?"

To the children's delight, the man said he did have some information on the subject. He went to a desk and pulled out a wide envelope containing colorful papers.

"Here's one," he said and showed them a picture of a tall boxlike structure. "This is what is played to make the carillon bells ring. There are others that look like big church organs with keyboards. The player makes the keys swing the hammers. The boxes are easier to install, though. Some kinds have tape decks to play any kind of music."

Bert quickly interrupted. "Can any tape be used? Like a cassette or eight-track tape?"

Mr. Platt smiled. "No, the tapes are specially designed for each kind of equipment."

"In other words," put in Nan, "if someone wanted to play his own music on another person's carillon, he would have to use his tapes."

Bert did not know how the eerie-sounding music of the Silver Town Mint Carillon fitted into their mystery. But he was convinced it had something to do with it. He and Freddie had heard the carillon play when, according to Papa Lasky, it was not supposed to.

Now a mysterious meeting between Mr. Lasky and someone else was scheduled to take place at the mint!

Presently the twins thanked the store owner for his help and said good-by.

"Any time," he replied. "Why don't you keep this carillon ad? I have extras. Compliments of Platt's Pied Piper Shop!"

From there the Bobbseys decided to stop at the post office to inquire about the box-number address on the package. Inside, a short line of people stood at one counter. The rest of it was closed temporarily.

"My feet hurt!" Flossie complained as they found themselves behind a man with a sack of packages. She peered at the bulging canvas. "He'll take forever," she whispered.

Hearing her voice, the man in front shifted closer to the person ahead. From the side, Bert thought he recognized him. He nudged Nan. Yes, he was the inspector from the "clean room" at the mint, the one who had accused her of trying to steal a medal die!

The children remained directly behind the

man, hoping he would not discover them right away. Why was he delivering so many packages? Was that part of his job for the company?

As his turn came, the man lifted the bulging sack onto the counter. A couple of small boxes fell out. Bert strained his neck to see what was written on them. "Silver Town Mint," he read, but could not see any more.

"You just made it," the friendly man behind the counter said to the fellow. "The mail truck is getting ready to leave. Is everything sorted as usual?"

The man nodded. Immediately the clerk handed the sack to a uniformed driver, who whisked it out a side exit.

Bert edged forward, disappointed that he had not had another look at the small package. "Can you tell me who has this box number?" he asked the clerk. He showed him a piece of paper on which he had written the return address on the mysterious package the twins had received.

The clerk stared at it briefly. "I can't give out any information. That's strictly confidential," he said, much to Bert's chagrin.

The younger twins had also recognized the scrawny employee of the Silver Town Mint. While Bert's and Nan's backs were turned, Freddie murmured something to Flossie, then slipped away.

The mail truck was parked in front of the post

office building. Short puffs of smoke were rising from the tailpipe. Through its open door the little boy could see several sacks of mail propped against one another.

"Maybe I can find out something about that man," he thought, and climbed up into the vehicle.

Immediately he went to a canvas bag through which corners of small cartons poked. He peeked inside. On top was a package with the same post-office-box return address as the one on the carton of the handbells!

CHAPTER XVI

FREDDIE DISAPPEARS

EXCITED by his discovery, Freddie wanted to leap out of the truck and tell his brother and sisters about it. But the side door clanged shut. A click told him he was locked in. It was dark.

The slow, idling engine sputtered. The vehicle rumbled out of the parking space and into the main street.

"Oh, no!" Freddie cried out.

He banged his hands against the sides of the vehicle, but it was useless. Nobody could hear him over the noisy motor.

"I'll get out at the next stop," he thought. He made a pillow of one of the softer sacks surrounding him and lay against it.

Inside the post office Bert was still trying to convince the mail clerk how important it was to the young detectives to trace the box number on their package. The clerk would not give any leads.

Using another angle, Bert asked about the person who had stood in front of him. "Does he always bring in sacks of packages from the Silver Town Mint Center?"

The clerk seemed annoyed by the boy's question. "Not always," he replied abruptly.

Bert would not give up. "I think it's odd that Silver Town Mint would ask an employee to carry a sack of packages here. Doesn't the post office usually pick up shipments from big firms?"

The man across the counter shifted nervously as the line behind the Bobbseys started to grow. "Yes," he said. "We do send a truck over there every day."

Standing alongside Bert, Nan spoke up, "If that's so, then why does that man from the mint come here?"

"Boy," the clerk said in a huffy manner, "I do not care why or who picks up or delivers which packages. Your guess is as good as mine. All I can tell you is that the fellow comes here often, Saturdays mostly, or late afternoon."

Bert was thrilled. The clerk had revealed something about the scrawny stranger!

Flossie could not see the top of the counter or

the clerk. She stood on tiptoe, trying to see him, but gave up. Fidgety, she twirled around and around. Her boots squeaked on the highly waxed floor. On the third go-round, Nan tugged on her to stop.

"I wish Freddie would come back," the little girl said.

Nan asked, "Where did he go, Flossie?"

The young twin stared out the front window of the building. The mail truck was gone and so was her brother!

"Nan, Nan," she said, excited, then told them the little boy's plan to examine the addresses on the packages from the Silver Town Mint.

Instantly Nan relayed the message to Bert, who was just turning away from the counter.

"What?" he asked. "He went where? How long ago?"

Neither sister had any idea but did not waste time making guesses. The three children dashed to the sidewalk, where a stream of people passed in front of them. Bert climbed up a tall mound of hardened snow next to a parking meter and looked down the street. Three or four stoplights ahead was a mail truck.

Sliding down the snow pile, he told Nan and Flossie what he had seen. "All the mail trucks look alike, though, so who knows if that's the one Freddie's in. Anyway, it's too late to catch it."

The mail truck was gone and so was Freddie!

"Now what are we going to do?" Flossie asked. "We'd better tell the post office."

When the mail clerk saw the children again, he breathed deeply. "Now what would you like to know?" he asked.

As fast as he could, Bert told him about Freddie's disappearance. "We're pretty sure he boarded the mail truck that left a little while ago."

A startled expression crossed the man's face. "He what?"

"Is there any way to contact the driver of the truck?" Bert asked.

"No, I'm afraid not."

"Do you know what his route is today?" was Bert's next question. Possibly the twins could call a few of the addresses where packages were to be delivered.

The clerk shook his head. "It's almost impossible to say exactly where that truck will make stops," he said. "Don't worry."

The children were astounded by the man's change of attitude.

"We have to find my twin!" said Flossie, ready to cry.

"You will, you will. I promise you," said the clerk. "All our trucks return here. Now what's your brother's full name?"

The little girl gave it, then spelled it out for

the man. "My name is Flossie and this is Bert and Nan. We're all the Bobbsey twins."

The mail clerk flashed a smile the children had not seen since he first greeted them. "I can see you're all related," he said, then asked for their home address and phone number.

As he jotted down the information, he said, "Your name rings a bell but I don't know why." He shrugged his shoulders. "Maybe you folks get a lot of mail!" he added, laughing.

The twins wondered if another surprise package for them might have passed over his counter recently.

"We'll see that Freddie gets home safely," the man promised, then nodded to the person behind Bert to come forward.

The twins, knowing there was nothing more they could do to find Freddie, discussed what they should do next. Bert suggested that he go to the mint by himself and try to find the scrawny man and talk to him.

Nan and Flossie were not in favor of this idea, however. "I don't think you ought to go to the carillon alone," said Nan. "Something might happen to you."

Bert dismissed the remark. "Like what?"

"Lots!" Flossie exclaimed.

Nan added, "Mother and Dad will be at the house. Tanya too. We should tell them."

Flossie stuck her mittened hand into Bert's. "We don't want to lose our other brother," she said.

As they stepped into the sunlight again, the children spotted a crosstown bus. It was letting passengers off and on at a corner. Waving to the driver, Bert led his sisters to the intersection. Shortly the three Bobbseys were seated together in the back of the bus.

The long vehicle pulled out into traffic. Flossie, who liked to sit by the window, peered out at the rows of stores decorated with broad banners. Some were plain white with a burst of stars on them. Others were red, white, and blue. All read:

LAKEPORT SALUTES AMERICA'S BIRTHDAY

Flossie tingled with excitement. She and the other children had often heard their mother and father say what a great country they lived in. Everybody in Lakeport felt the same way.

As she continued to gaze outside, a flash of blue and white passed by. Quickly the little girl climbed onto her seat and peered out the back window.

"Bert, it's a mail truck!" she exclaimed.

The bus driver had caught sight of the little girl in his rearview mirror. He shouted to her, "Please sit down before you get hurt!"

Nan pulled her sister back beside her. "There

are millions of mail trucks in the world," she said to Flossie. "Freddie is on only one of them."

When their street came into view, the twins moved to the front of the bus. The driver let them off at the corner, a short distance from the Bobbsey house.

Flossie stepped down first. She squealed in delight and ran through the slushy puddles on the sidewalk. "It's here. It's here. It's here!" she exclaimed happily.

Parked in front of their mother's car on the street was a mail truck.

"Freddie! Freddie!" his young sister called out, hoping her twin would appear.

Instead, a driver holding a brown paper wrapped package slid out of his seat.

The little girl halted. "He didn't bring Freddie!" she wailed. "We might never see him again!"

CHAPTER XVII

MORE MEAN TRICKS

As FLOSSIE spoke Freddie's name, the driver paused a second. Then he stepped into the mail truck. When he came out again, he was holding the little boy by the hand.

"Freddie! Freddie!" Flossie cried, dancing in her boots. "You're not missing any more!"

She hugged her twin while Nan and Bert said how happy they were to have him home.

The driver, who wore a quilted nylon jacket, was baffled. "How did you get in there?" he asked Freddie. "And what were you doing?"

The little boy told the man what had happened. "I didn't mean to stay inside," Freddie said. "But you shut the door before I could get out, and you didn't hear me banging and calling you."

The driver looked at the address on the package he was carrying. "Do you live here?" he asked, glancing at the house.

All the children said yes.

"Then your name is Bobbsey?" he asked. His listeners nodded. "You're lucky, son, that I had to make a stop at your house."

Freddie gazed into the man's eyes. "I knew you had to, 'cause I saw that box for Mommy," he said.

"For Mommy?" the others chorused. They thought that here might be another surprise gift, and possibly a clue, for them.

The four followed the man up the front walk. He rang the bell, which quickly brought Mrs. Bobbsey to the door.

"I have two packages for you, ma'am," he said.

He handed her the carton under his arm and then gestured to Freddie. "I'm sure you must've been worried about him, missing all this time!"

"Missing?" she repeated, wondering what the man was talking about. "Will somebody please explain?" She looked at the older twins for an answer.

Instead, the truck driver replied, "He was taking a nap in my mail truck."

"In the mail truck?" Mrs. Bobbsey gasped.

Before she could say another word, the man turned away. "I must hurry," he said. "I have many more calls to make."

"But—— But——" Mrs. Bobbsey tried to stop him, but he did not wait for her to thank him.

When the children went inside, they took off their outer clothing. The twins were eager to see the contents of their mother's package, but she insisted that first they tell her of their adventure downtown.

Tanya, hearing the chatter of voices, entered the room. Her eyes looked puffy, perhaps from crying. "I had a wonderful sleep," she said, but Mrs. Bobbsey wondered if the girl felt well.

Tanya plopped into the chair her American father had sat in earlier. "Did I miss much?" she asked.

The twins giggled and recounted their experiences of the morning. But they kept looking constantly at the box on Mrs. Bobbsey's lap. Finally she started to open it.

"I ordered this a while ago and almost gave up hope that it would ever come," she said, letting the brown paper wrapping fall to the rug. Flossie reached for it.

"Oh!" she cried out. "Mommy got something from the box number!"

She passed the paper to the others. Indeed, the

return address on it was the Silver Town Mint Center!

Bert teased, "Why didn't you tell us you had ordered something from the mint?"

She grinned and said, "You never asked me." The children laughed.

His mother opened the box and took out a silvery disk from a plastic envelope. She turned it around for all to see.

"Isn't it lovely? The mint is going to make a whole series of special patriotic things to honor the birth of America. This is the first one."

Bert shocked her by declaring, "I'll bet it isn't real!" He went on to explain why he thought so. "We think that box number has been set up by a bunch of phonies who work for the company!"

Tanya blinked at the remark. "Your mother has been tricked too?"

The twin detectives said they were not positive of this, since they were not experts on silver. Bert studied the piece. "It looks like pure silver, but maybe another metal was substituted and only coated with silver to make it look more valuable."

"I'd like to take this to the mint, Mother," he said, "and compare it with others on display in the museum."

"You may go right after lunch," Mrs. Bobbsey said, looking at her watch.

Dinah had prepared a crock of steaming, home-

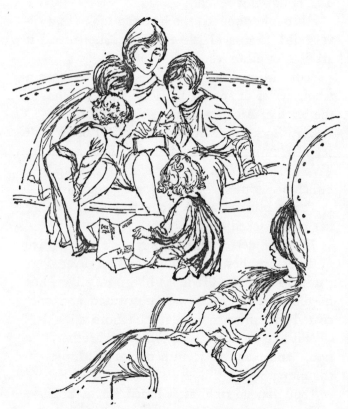

The return address was the Silver Town Mint Center!

made soup and a variety of meat and cheese sand-
wiches.

"I made something *real* special for you today,"
the plump woman said with a chuckle. "It's a
chocolate riddle!"

She took an oval dish from the refrigerator. On
it lay a cream-filled chocolate-roll cake with soft,
tiny chocolate sprinkles on top. It was filled with
whipped cream.

"Are those candy riddles?" Flossie asked.

Dinah gently lifted the dessert onto a wooden
board. "Mm-hmm! I got the recipe from a detective like you," Dinah replied mysteriously. "She's
a little bit older than you are."

The small twin was befuddled. "Who is she?"
Flossie asked quickly.

As Dinah sliced off the end of the chocolate
roll, she said, "Why, Nancy Drew, honey. I found
her cookbook the other day."

"Oh really?" Nan said. "Where?"

Dinah cut several large pieces from the cream-
filled roll and said, "I bought the *Nancy Drew
Cookbook* in a big bookstore. It's full of mysteries
like this one. And the recipes are mighty simple
to follow. Anybody can make 'em."

The twins promised to spend some time with
Dinah in the kitchen as soon as they finished
working on their Freedom Bell case.

"Do you suppose we could take our dessert

with us to the mint?" Bert asked, checking his watch.

Mrs. Bobbsey said it would be all right. "But wrap each piece carefully so it won't spill."

Within the hour the four twins, carrying their slices of cake wrapped in foil, arrived at the mint. It was still surrounded by thick snow. The carillon was playing a tuneful melody.

"That sounds bee-yoo-ti-ful!" Flossie remarked.

As the twins approached the main entrance to the museum, the broad glass door rolled back automatically. No one seemed to be around.

Quietly the children climbed a nearby flight of steps to a corridor where the lighting was dim. At the end of it was a wooden door marked PRIVATE—CARILLON.

"The carillon must be played in that room," Nan whispered to the others. "Let's take a look."

She tiptoed down the hall with Bert, Freddie, and Flossie close behind. Nan cupped her hand over the knob and turned it slowly. The door was not locked!

Nan glanced at her brothers and sister for their signal to open it. Shivering, Flossie nodded. Then Bert and Freddie gave their okay.

Without squeaking or groaning, the door began to open. Through the crack the twins could see a tall metal box with dials on it. The box looked like the picture Mr. Platt had shown them.

At the instrument stood a man who wore a heavy wool cape that hid the size of his body. A knit cap covered his hair. He switched off the electric current that made the carillon play.

The man removed a tape, then slipped in another one, and set the dial. Now he turned the current back on. Eerie, haunting sounds floated into the hallway. Was he testing the tape for later use? the twins wondered.

Flossie clung to Nan, who patted her little sister's shoulder. But no one spoke.

Meanwhile, Freddie had stripped off part of the aluminum foil covering the cake he had brought and munched a piece. The stranger heard the soft rustle of paper but ignored it. Then Flossie sneezed. The man swiveled, revealing his bony features!

"Oh!" the children cried, as the evil-faced man flung his cape open and stalked toward them.

"I'll take care of you once and for all!" he cried out, and shook his long skinny forefinger at the Bobbseys.

The younger twins screamed and started to race down the hallway toward the steps. Nan and Bert followed. Freddie clutched his piece of cake tightly. Some cream squirted out onto the floor but the goo did not stop their pursuer. His cape flapping, he tore after the twins like a giant bird.

The children stumbled down the narrow stairway, but were stopped midway by two men climbing up. The red-haired twins!

"Going somewhere?" one of them asked. He spread his muscular arms to block their escape.

The pair eased up the stairway. The twins' hearts were pounding, and a thousand thoughts raced through their minds. They were forced to reclimb the steps. At the top the third man waited to pounce on them.

As they neared the landing, Freddie and Flossie tried to slip past the man's cape, which hung like a black curtain in front of them. But he grabbed their coat collars with his icy fingers and shoved them toward the carillon room.

"You can't get away from me now!" he snarled.

The other two took charge of Nan and Bert, pushing them down the dark corridor.

"Did Lasky tip you off?" one of the men buzzed into Bert's ear.

The boy squirmed under the man's heavy breathing but did not respond.

"I'm talking to you, kid!" his captor growled.

The man who resembled him cut his partner short. "Aw, leave him alone. He's just a baby!"

Bert clenched his teeth. "I'm no baby," he thought, and wished for a chance to trap the men and prove otherwise.

As the brothers took him and Nan into the carillon room, the men talked openly. "I thought you scared these kids off permanently when you rolled those silver carts at 'em," one said to the other.

Although the other man's voice was a bit lower, the children could not tell the men apart. At first the second one did not reply. But finally he said, "I'm looking for something to tie up these snoopy kids. I didn't plan on bumpin' into the Bobbseys again," he mumbled. "When I saw the boys near Lasky's place the night of the snowstorm, I knew it meant trouble."

The third man interrupted. "Just because you read about their little mystery adventures in the local paper, you thought they'd find out about our setup."

"There ain't no rope or nothin' around here," one of the red-haired twins replied. "Why did *you* pick such a dumb place to meet Lasky?"

Ignoring the remark, the birdlike gang member went on with his work. He loosened Nan's and Bert's coats.

"If you two hadn't played tricks on the Bobbseys, they wouldn't have caught on to us at all," he said.

In the meantime, the man in the cape, who seemed to be the leader of the gang flung his cape behind his shoulders. He placed his bony fingers on the buttons of Freddie's coat.

The little boy jumped back. In a flash he hurled his gooey dessert into the face of his attacker.

Instantly Flossie aimed her own piece of cake at the man. She hit his nose and eyes squarely with the cream-filling and squashy chocolate sprinkles.

CHAPTER XVIII

THE RESCUE

BEFORE either of the red-haired men could tie the twins up, Nan and Bert acted. They flung their whipped cream desserts at the other two captors. Goo dripped down their foreheads and over their eyes as they stumbled blindly after the children.

"I'll get you!" the man in the cape yelled, wiping his eyes. But as he rubbed them, the whipped cream seeped under his lids. Now he could not see anything.

Freddie and Flossie screeched as he tried to grab them. Nan and Bert dashed for the door that had latched shut.

"Let's get out of here!" Bert cried, taking his sisters' hands. Freddie was at their heels.

The birdlike man followed the sound of the children's footsteps. In a moment he circled the little boy with a powerful sweep of his arms.

"Help! Help!" Freddie yelled.

Suddenly the door burst open. In came Papa Lasky! He was carrying a paper bag.

"Take your hands off that boy!" he roared at the man, who squinted at him through the cream in his eyes.

One of the red-haired men heard the rustle of the bag near him and tried to wrench it away. "Give me that!" he ordered sharply.

Papa Lasky threw it to Bert. The boy quickly stowed it in a corner, then sent a flying fist to the man's jaw. His red-haired partner stumbled to help him, swinging his arms at Papa Lasky.

He missed him, hitting his brother instead. The angry man whirled and returned the blow. Both men staggered dizzily to the floor.

Nan grabbed the tape from the carillon and broke the cartridge open. As the tape unwound, she threw it around the brothers, tangling them in a web from which they could not escape for a while.

"That's it, Nan!" Flossie cheered. Imitating what her sister had done, the little girl seized the cape on the third man and pulled one end of it around his spindly legs.

"Take your hands off that boy!" Papa Lasky roared.

His clawlike hand brushed at her. "Let go!" he exclaimed, yanking at his cape.

Freddie at last was able to slip from the man's grasp and now grabbed the other end of the cape. He held the material tightly and swung it around the man.

While Papa Lasky and Nan held the red-haired brothers in tow, Bert darted to his younger brother and sister. He tied the ends of the ample cape in a double knot, pinning the man's arms to his body. At last he was trapped!

The Bobbseys used their long scarves and the sleeves of their coats, which they removed. The four young detectives bound the red-haired strangers with them. As a final precaution, they led the third member to the carillon and tied his ankles to the legs of the heavy metal instrument.

"That ought to keep you here until the police arrive," Bert declared.

In the distance a police siren blared. It grew louder by the second. Papa Lasky said he had contacted headquarters before leaving home.

"These creeps thought I would make a deal with them," he revealed. "They figured I would be part of their crooked schemes because I was out of work. They said they could use an extra engraver. As if I would do anything so underhanded——"

The sound of running footsteps on the corridor floor interrupted him for a moment. "I don't know why they thought I would be so stupid or why they wanted that useless piece of junk," he added, motioning to the crumpled bag that lay a few feet away. "But they insisted that I bring it."

Bert picked up the bag and removed the silver plate with the Liberty Bell engraved on it. He seemed to be measuring the thickness of the object with his fingers. "I think I know why!" he exclaimed, and dropped the plate.

As the dish splintered, the door swung wide. Four policemen rushed in, ready for battle with any wrongdoers. When they saw the Bobbseys and Mr. Lasky with their prisoners bound up and a mess of whipped-cream and chocolate, one of the officers howled with laughter.

"What a sight!" he exclaimed. "And you beat us to the punch again!"

A second policeman glanced at Bert and the broken plate. "You have quite a temper, my boy!" he commented.

Bert denied it with a chuckle. "No, sir," he said. "I just had a hunch!"

He peeled off what appeared to be a thick silvery coating on the object. Revealed beneath was a dull-gray plate with a faint scroll design on the rim. Engraved in the center was the Liberty Bell!

"Amazing!" Papa Lasky exclaimed. "It's the silver plate that was stolen from the Lakeport Museum!"

The boy detective beamed.

"Bee-yoo-ti-ful!" Flossie put in.

"When it's shined up," Nan said, "it will be even prettier."

Papa Lasky's mouth fell open. "But how did you know, Bert?"

While the policemen listened to the twins' explanation, they exchanged the children's coat sleeves and scarves on the men for handcuffs.

"We know, Mr. Lasky, that somebody had ransacked your attic," Bert said. "Why? Because he was looking for something. You said the plate was the only item left by the previous occupant of your house.

"When I happened to see another copy of this plate on display at the museum, it seemed to be just a bit thinner than yours. Of course, I wasn't positive of that. You made sure Tanya didn't take the plate with her to our house so this was my first chance to study it again."

As he glanced at the scroll mark carved lightly on the rim, Bert concluded, "I guess the coating was too thick to pick up the fine details of this design."

The policemen wiped the goo off their prisoners' faces while the three men argued with one another.

"You idiots!" the birdman screeched at his partners. He gazed sadly at the cracked mold on the floor. "My beautiful formula!"

He admitted that he had lived in the Lasky home when he first moved to the Silver Town section. "My relatives on the other side of Lakeport owned the house. They kicked me out because they didn't like some of the people I hung around with, including these two."

He went on to say that he had stolen the silver plate, among other things, from the museum before he became involved in the present scheme.

"Remember, you're the great artist, Widget," one of the red-haired men put in sarcastically.

The gang member's name was Widget! "Are you related to Miss Widget, who teaches at Fairfield School?" Nan asked him, now seeing the resemblance.

The man shifted uneasily. "Yes," he said. "She's my half-sister. Tried to make me change my ways but I guess I'm just no good."

"No wonder the second-grade teacher was nervous!" the Bobbseys thought.

Flossie spoke up. "Miss Widget's a nice lady. We like her a lot," she said. "You could be a nice man too!"

For an instant the hardened expression in Widget's eyes softened. Perhaps, the Bobbseys thought, he could be helped to become a worthwhile citizen.

"It's all their fault," he said, pointing at the red-haired brothers.

He said they had worked at the Silver Town

Mint Center for a while and had convinced their friend to apply for a job also.

"We stole some ideas from Lasky and a few others at the plant and developed a formula that looked and felt like silver," one admitted. "Most people aren't experts on the stuff. We fooled 'em."

Nan commented that most of the Silver Town Mint collectors were smarter than he supposed. "Did you really think you could keep selling fakes to buyers without ever being caught?" she asked.

The spokesman for the brothers replied, "We didn't plan to stay around too long after we took in all the money. We were going to another private minting company in the Midwest to pull the same thing."

He explained that they had copied the company's customer mailing lists. "We set up a post office box number so nobody could trace us, then sent every subscriber announcements of our items for sale and order blanks with the new address. As soon as we got in each request and the money, we mailed our merchandise."

Freddie wanted to know about the carton of handbells. "Did you send them to us?" he asked.

The man in the cape said yes. "A little gift from a church-choir room," he added.

"You stole the bells from a church?" Flossie gasped.

The prisoner snickered. "Why not?" he replied. "Did you enjoy my little joke?"

Flossie shook her head, which made him laugh. "I decided to bake one of the bells in my formula. Didn't you have fun trying to ring it?"

His question went unanswered as Freddie inquired about the weird-sounding tape that had been played on the carillon.

"We used that as a signal," Widget said. "We got a couple of other guys from the mint to work with us. If you had been smart, Lasky——" he paused, then returned to the subject. "Whenever we planned to make a delivery or have some of the phony goods picked up, naturally we didn't want to use company phones. It was easy to switch tapes and reset the timer on the carillon."

The policemen said the others involved in the scheme would be arrested shortly.

In the meantime, another question occurred to Bert. "Is the van with the bell painted on the back of it yours?"

The trio confessed that it was. "Too bad we didn't make permanent snowmen out of you two," one of the red-haired brothers declared.

"Too bad your truck didn't look like a real telephone repair truck," Freddie returned.

Bert added, "Your hideout must've been right around the corner from the Laskys'."

Widget explained that the other two men had

rented a house on a nearby street. For the sake of convenience and protection, he had moved in with them.

Flossie cuddled up to Papa Lasky. "I'm glad I keep my ears open, even when my nose is stuffed up!"

The stocky man laughed heartily. "So you heard what was said on the phone." He slapped his knees. "That's how you knew I was coming here. Well, you are fantastic children!"

One of the policemen nudged him. "The chief thinks so too!" he said, grinning.

When the Bobbseys reached home with Papa Lasky, they were greeted by Tanya. For an hour the twins held her, their parents, and Dinah spellbound by the story of the rescue and capture.

"Oh, Papa, how wonderful!" Tanya cried joyfully. "You will be able to go back to work, and I will stay in the United States of America!"

The next day the twins went to church and prayed with thankful hearts that Tanya would not have to return to her troubled country. "And bless Mr. Widget too. You can help him, God, even if we and Miss Widget can't," Flossie added.

Within a few weeks the entire Bobbsey family, the Laskys, and Tanya were invited to be guests of honor at a special party at the Silver Town Mint. The main lobby of the building had been turned into a festive hall decorated with colorful banners of red and white roses braided with blue ribbon. Beneath them at long tables sat hundreds of employees and townspeople.

The twins spotted Mr. Platt in their midst and waved. He gave the children a broad smile as they walked to the head table. The Mayor of Lakeport, the president of the company, and the curator of the museum were seated there.

When the twins took their places, everyone in the room rose to his feet. They clapped for several minutes, then sat down when the president of the firm stepped to a microphone. He asked Nan, Flossie, Freddie, and Bert to stand up.

"These children are a tribute to America," he began.

Mr. and Mrs. Bobbsey stirred with pride as the words rang out and loud applause followed.

"I want to present each of you twins with your very own medals," the president went on. He handed out gleaming silver disks on which their portraits had been engraved along with the wonderful words he had spoken.

Flossie rubbed her small fingers over the highly polished letters. "They're going to stay forever, just like Tanya!" she said.

Then came the biggest surprise of the evening. The Mayor of Lakeport, holding a small gold key, went to the microphone. "Mr. and Mrs. Mirov, will you please come in now?"

Weeping and smiling at the same time, Tanya's parents were escorted to the table. A joyous reunion with their amazed daughter followed. In their native tongue the couple told Tanya that the Silver Town Mint Center had arranged for them to come to the U.S.A. through government connections.

The Mayor slipped welcoming arms around the Mirovs and gave them the key to the city. "This will open new doors for you!" he said. "Because of the work of these Bobbsey twins you will live in freedom!"

The bells of the carillon rang out, then played "My Country 'Tis of Thee." Everyone sang:

> *My country 'tis of thee,*
> *Sweet land of liberty,*
> *Of thee I sing;*
> *Land where my fathers died,*
> *Land of the pilgrims' pride,*
> *From every mountainside*
> *Let freedom ring.*

When the music finished, Flossie gazed up into the tearful eyes of Tanya's mother and father. "Do you know what that is?" she asked as the final bell pealed.

Although the woman did not understand much English, she nodded warmly at the little girl. Then she shrugged as if to say, "I don't know."

Flossie pulled the microphone down to her level and replied for all to hear, "That's your freedom bell!"